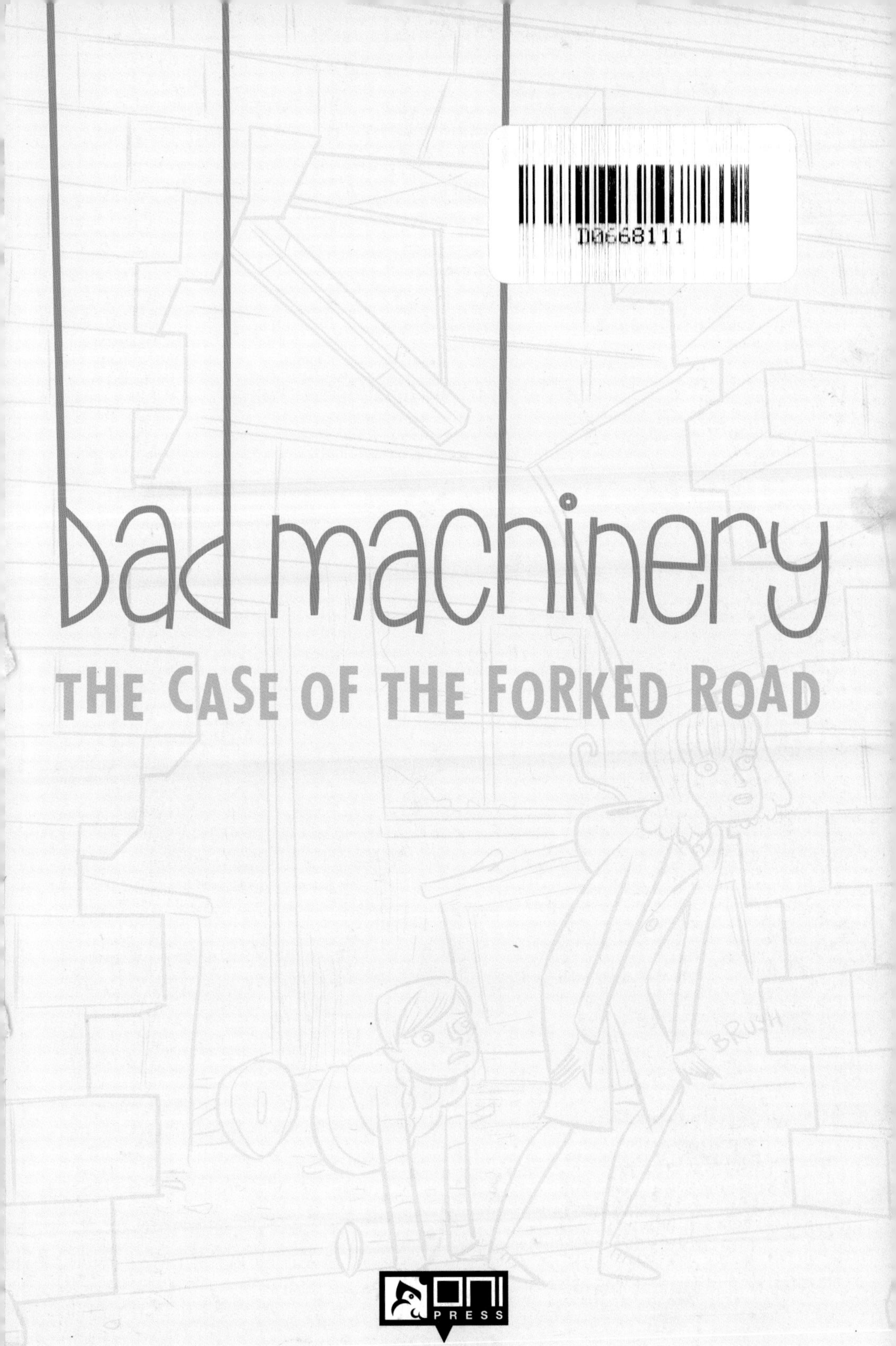
BRUSH

bad machinery

THE CASE OF THE FORKED ROAD

ONI PRESS

AN ONI PRESS PUBLICATION

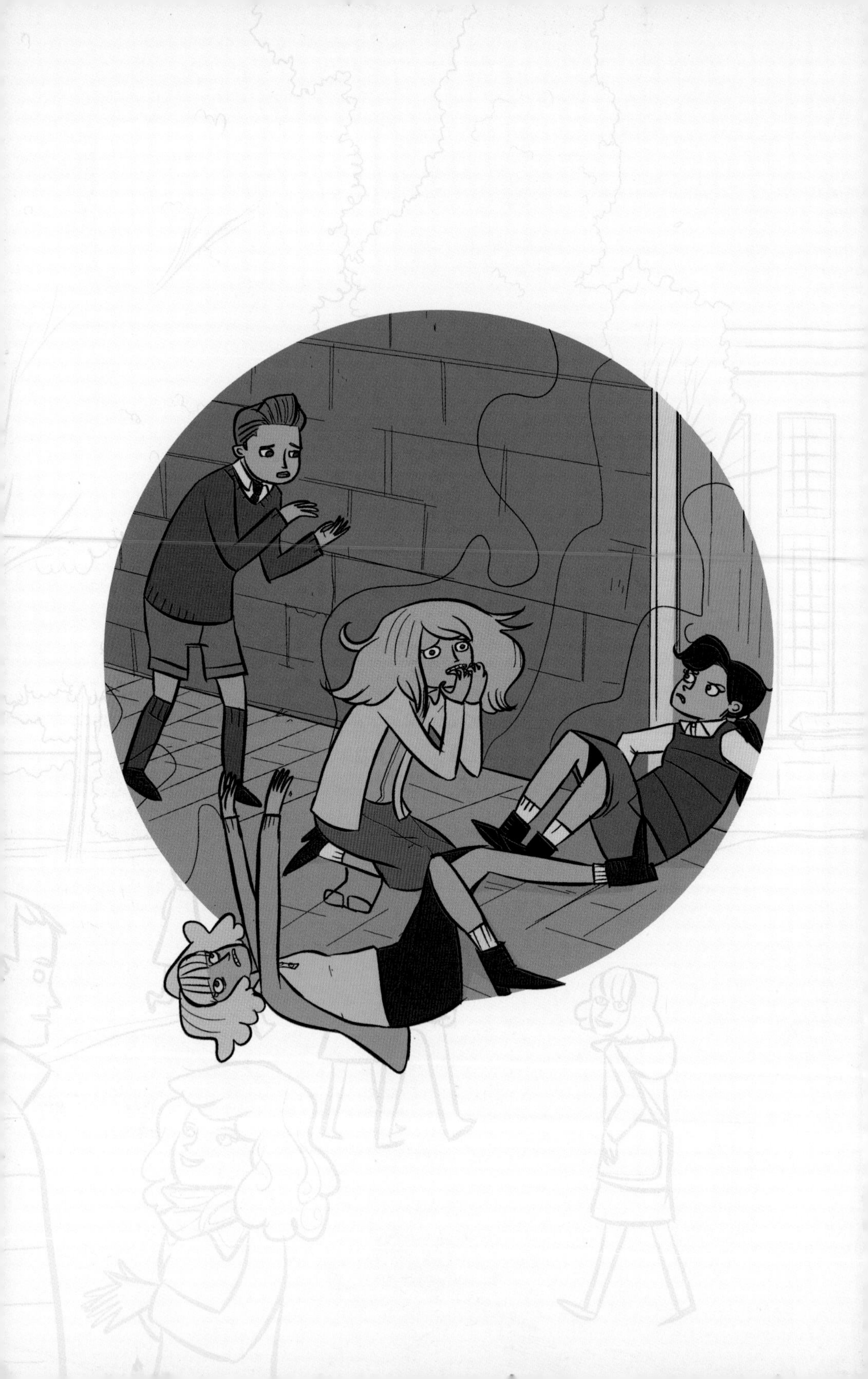

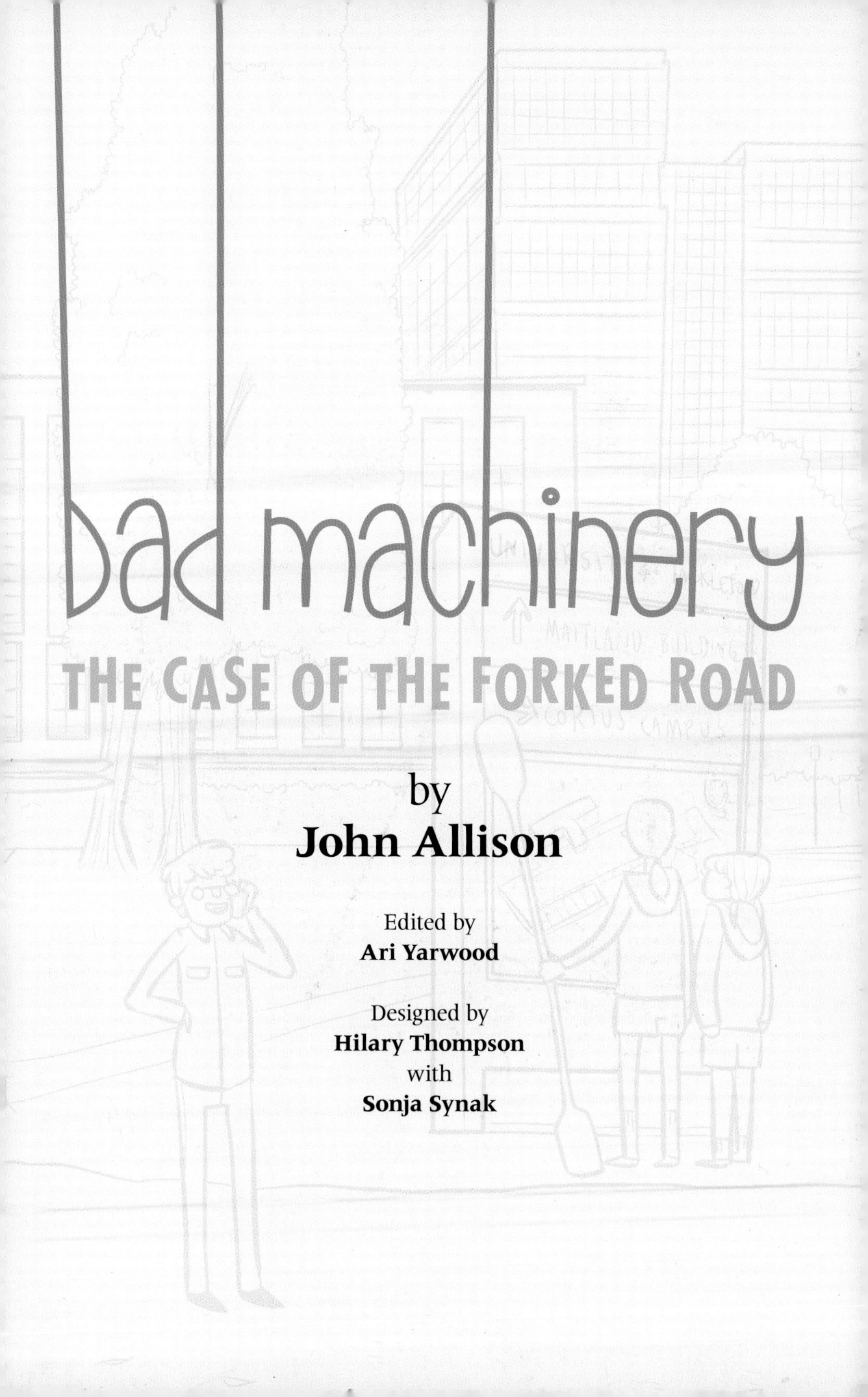
MAITLAND BUILDING
CORTUS CAMPUS

Bad Machinery

The Case of the Forked Road

by

John Allison

Edited by
Ari Yarwood

Designed by
Hilary Thompson
with
Sonja Synak

PUBLISHED BY ONI PRESS INC.

Joe Nozemack, *founder & chief financial officer*
James Lucas Jones, *publisher*
Charlie Chu, *v.p. of creative & business development*
Brad Rooks, *director of operations*
Melissa Meszaros, *director of publicity*
Margot Wood, *director of sales*
Sandy Tanaka, *marketing design manager*
Amber O'Neill, *special projects manager*
Troy Look, *director of design & production*
Kate Z. Stone, *graphic designer*
Sonja Synak, *graphic designer*
Angie Knowles, *digital prepress lead*
Ari Yarwood, *executive editor*
Sarah Gaydos, *editorial director of licensed publishing*
Robin Herrera, *senior editor*
Desiree Wilson, *associate editor*
Michelle Nguyen, *executive assistant*
Jung Lee, *logistics associate*
Scott Sharkey, *warehouse assistant*

onipress.com
facebook.com/onipress
twitter.com/onipress
onipress.tumblr.com
instagram.com/onipress
scarygoround.com

FIRST EDITION: MAY 2017
POCKET EDITION: JANUARY 2019

ISBN 978-1-62010-562-7
EISBN 978-1-62010-391-3

BAD MACHINERY VOLUME SEVEN: THE CASE OF THE FORKED ROAD, POCKET EDITION. JANUARY 2019. PUBLISHED BY ONI PRESS, INC. 1319 SE MARTIN LUTHER KING JR. BLVD., SUITE 240, PORTLAND, OR 97214.

PRINTED IN CHINA.

LIBRARY OF CONGRESS CONTROL NUMBER: 2018950254

1 2 3 4 5 6 7 8 9 10

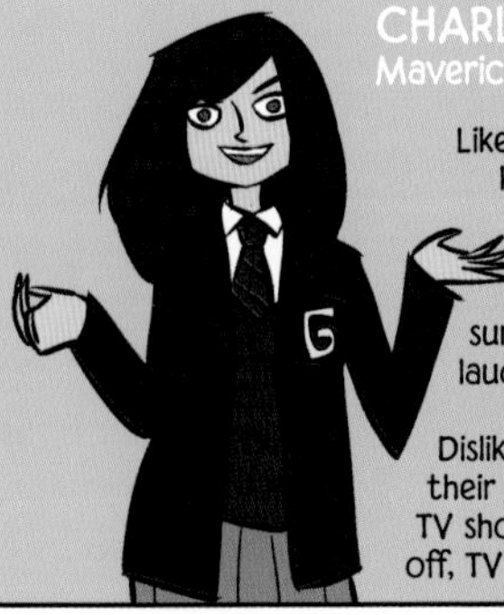

CHARLOTTE GROTE
Maverick, profile writer

Likes: who can truly know my heart? Only I dear reader hem hem. I like mystery, and trouble. A summer's day. A baby's laugh. Pumpkin seeds!

Dislikes: when people put their shoes on the bed in TV shows. Take your shoes off, TV characters!

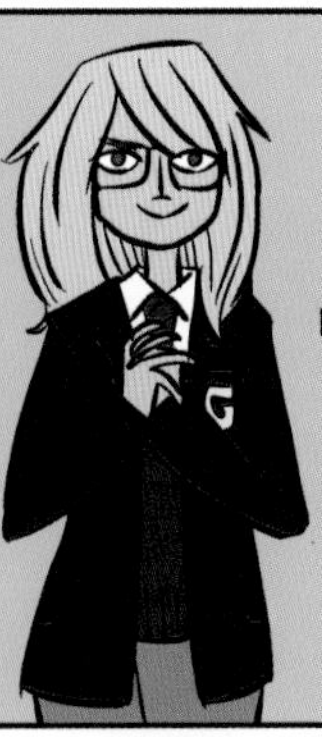

SHAUNA WICKLE
BFF (M/W/F/Su)

Likes: academic excellence, avoiding the glare of authority.

Dislikes: people who don't undertand brutalist architecture. "It's meant to look like that" she says. It looks like a big grey box to me but whatevs.

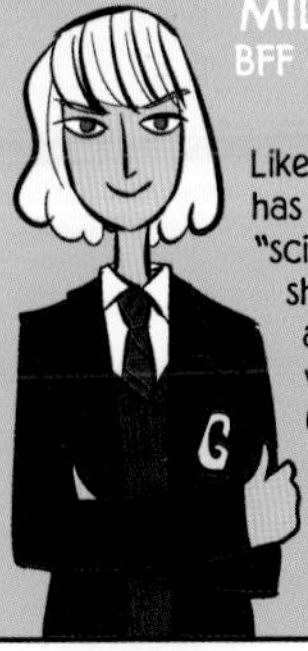

MILDRED HAVERSHAM
BFF (Tu/Th/Sa)

Likes: Mildred has a perverse interest in "science" and half the stuff she comes out with sounds at best well spurious and worst specially designed (by her) to fool the gullible eg me, *la Grote.*

Dislikes: enforced, lifelong veganism.

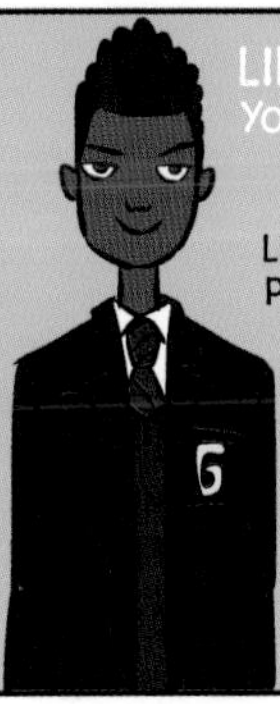

LINTON BAXTER
Youth sleuth

Likes: being right, all the time. Probably likes men's football and other typical man's things eg underground fight clubs and steaks.

Dislikes: being proved wrong and any subsequent victory celebrations.

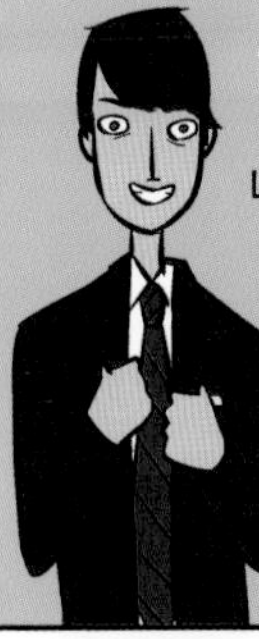

JACK FINCH
Basic detective

Likes: the ladies. Jack is away with the fairies all the time thinking about whatever dame has crossed his path with her floral "scent" an enchanting "ways".

Dislikes: Jack has broad tastes but he doesn't have much time for moths.

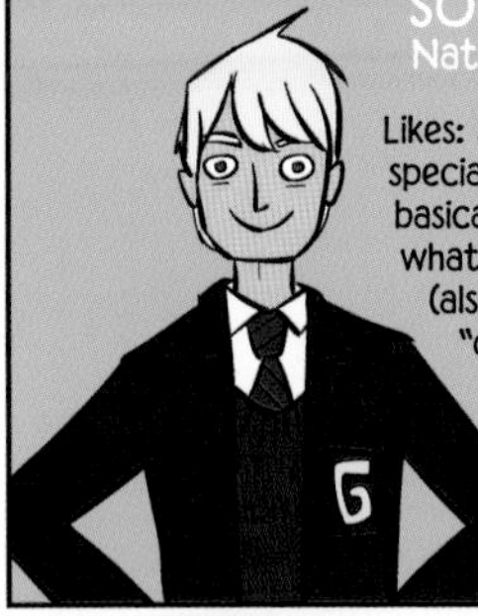

SONNY CRAVEN
Naturally kind

Likes: Sonny is our angel, our special boy. His way of being basically decent in a world what is always getting darker (also perhaps "grim" and "gritty") suggests that he likes almost everything that is good in this world.

Dislikes: EVIL.

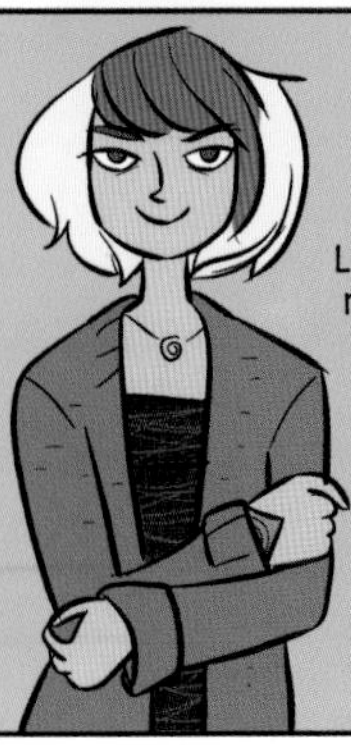

AMY BECKWITH-CHILTON
Sassy antiques expert?

Likes : ABC's likes are a mystery to me but seeing as how she has got mad tattoos all along both arms I guess she likes pain and Mr Harley Davidson's motorbikes.

Dislikes: I reckon she dislikes conformity and THE MAN.

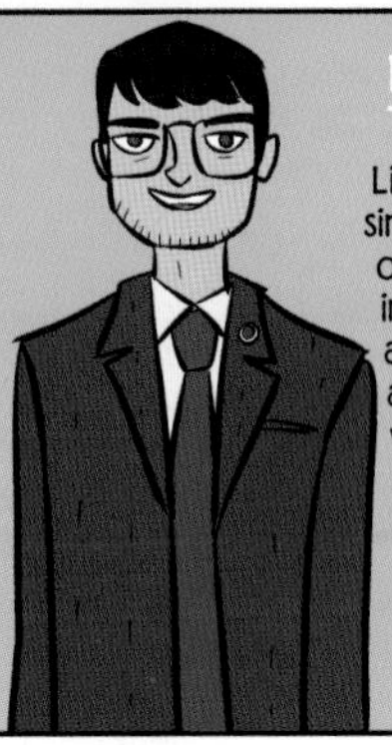

RYAN BECKWITH
Teacher, husband, tired

Likes: Mr Beckwith is a simple soul who likes a cup of bad instant coffee, quiet in the classroom, and us not asking him questions that are maybe not related to what he is teaching us about. Also he probably likes his well nice wife.

Dislikes: there is a rumour that he once karate chopped a snake.

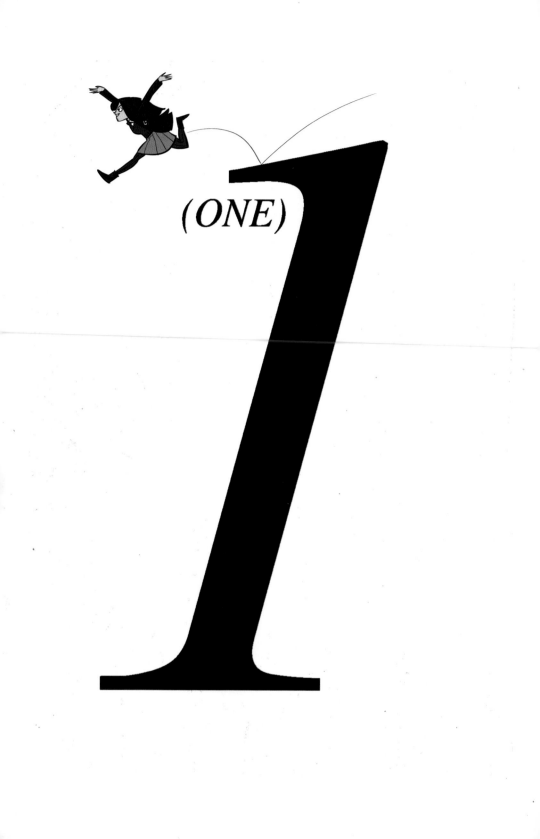

(ONE)

1

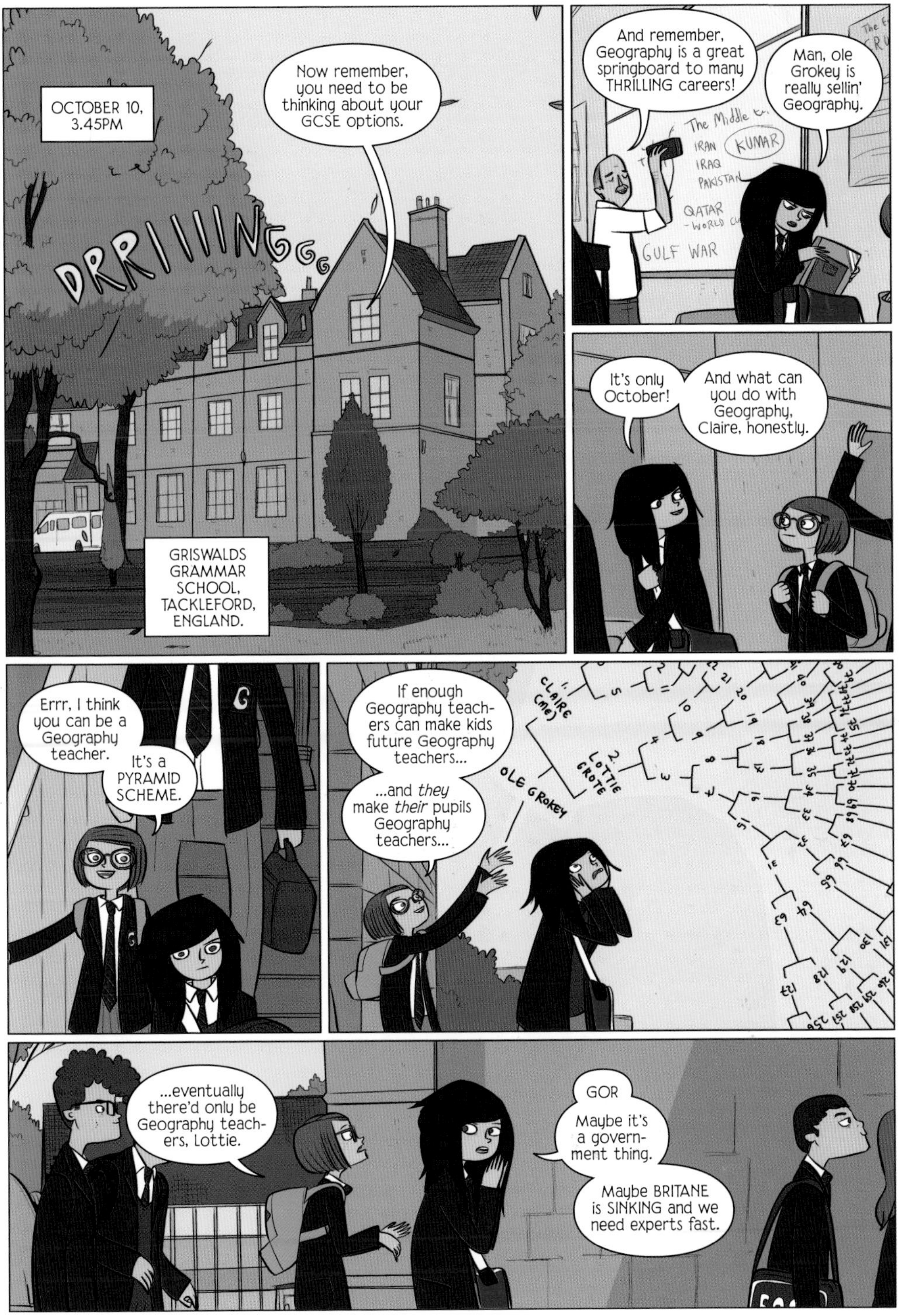
OCTOBER 10, 3.45PM
Now remember, you need to be thinking about your GCSE options.
DRRIIIINGGG
GRISWALDS GRAMMAR SCHOOL, TACKLEFORD, ENGLAND.
And remember, Geography is a great springboard to many THRILLING careers!
The Middle E...
IRAN
KUMAR
IRAQ
PAKISTAN
QATAR
- WORLD CU...
GULF WAR
Man, ole Grokey is really sellin' Geography.
It's only October!
And what can you do with Geography, Claire, honestly.
Errr, I think you can be a Geography teacher.
It's a PYRAMID SCHEME.
If enough Geography teachers can make kids future Geography teachers...
...and *they* make *their* pupils Geography teachers...
OLE GROKEY
1. CLAIRE (ME)
2. LOTTIE GROTE
...eventually there'd only be Geography teachers, Lottie.
GOR
Maybe it's a government thing.
Maybe BRITANE is SINKING and we need experts fast.

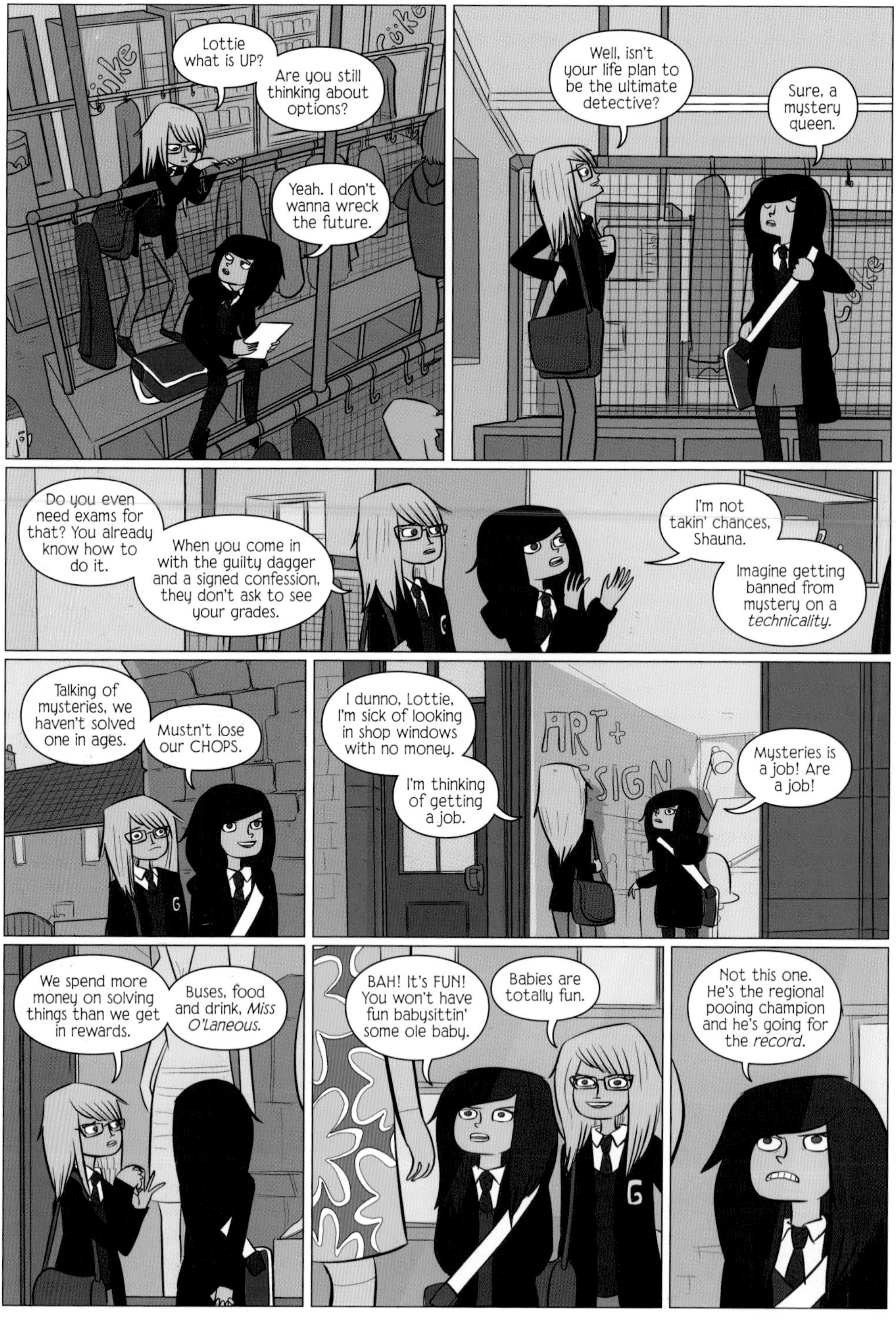
Lottie what is UP?
Are you still thinking about options?
Yeah. I don't wanna wreck the future.
Well, isn't your life plan to be the ultimate detective?
Sure, a mystery queen.
Do you even need exams for that? You already know how to do it.
When you come in with the guilty dagger and a signed confession, they don't ask to see your grades.
I'm not takin' chances, Shauna.
Imagine getting banned from mystery on a *technicality.*
Talking of mysteries, we haven't solved one in ages.
Mustn't lose our CHOPS.
I dunno, Lottie, I'm sick of looking in shop windows with no money.
I'm thinking of getting a job.
ART + DESIGN
Mysteries is a job! Are a job!
We spend more money on solving things than we get in rewards.
Buses, food and drink, *Miss O'Laneous.*
BAH! It's FUN! You won't have fun babysittin' some ole baby.
Babies are totally fun.
Not this one. He's the regional pooing champion and he's going for the *record.*

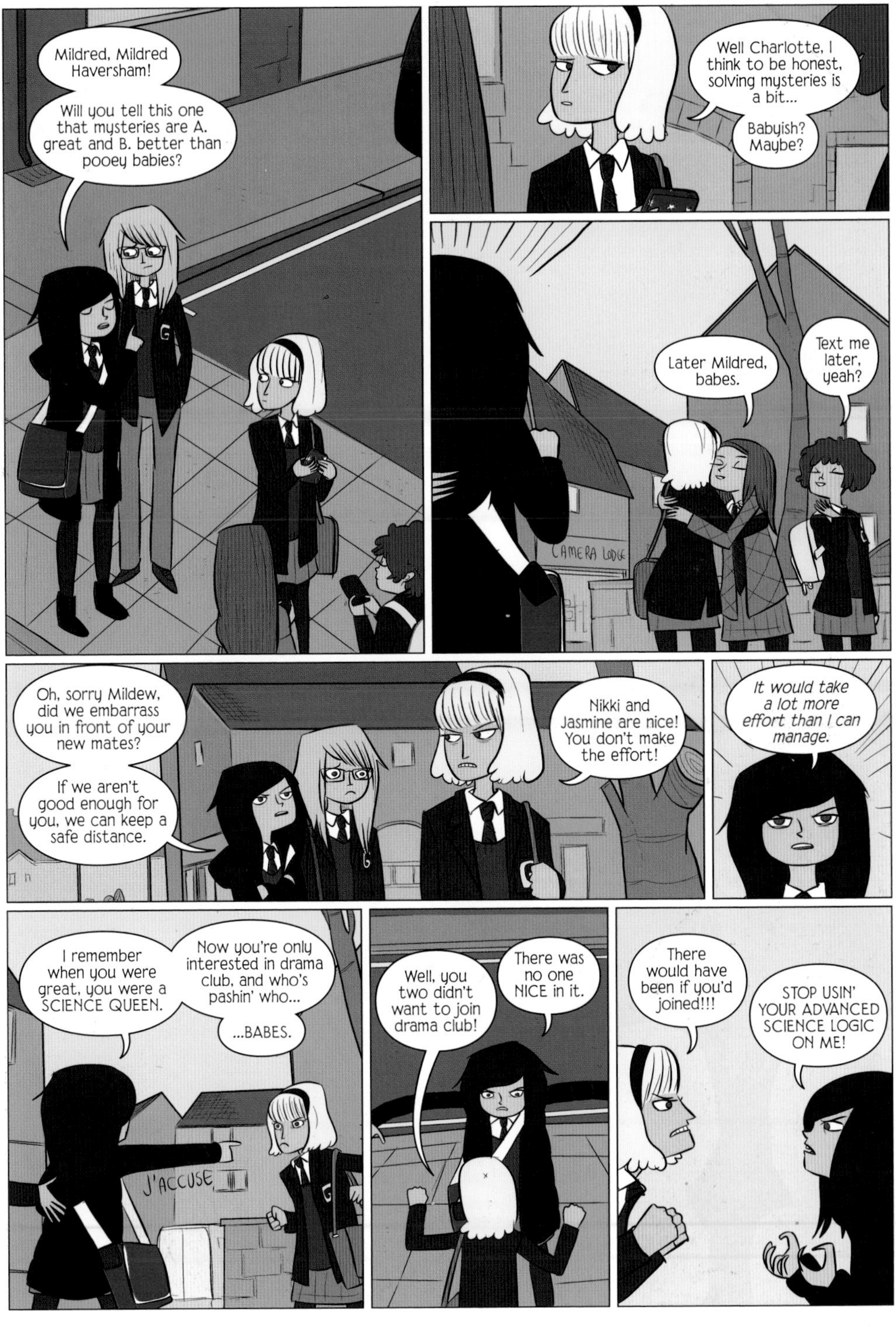
Mildred, Mildred Haversham!
Will you tell this one that mysteries are A. great and B. better than pooey babies?
Well Charlotte, I think to be honest, solving mysteries is a bit...
Babyish? Maybe?
Later Mildred, babes.
Text me later, yeah?
CAMERA LODGE
Oh, sorry Mildew, did we embarrass you in front of your new mates?
If we aren't good enough for you, we can keep a safe distance.
Nikki and Jasmine are nice! You don't make the effort!
It would take a lot more effort than I can manage.
I remember when you were great, you were a SCIENCE QUEEN.
Now you're only interested in drama club, and who's pashin' who...
...BABES.
J'ACCUSE
Well, you two didn't want to join drama club!
There was no one NICE in it.
There would have been if you'd joined!!!
STOP USIN' YOUR ADVANCED SCIENCE LOGIC ON ME!

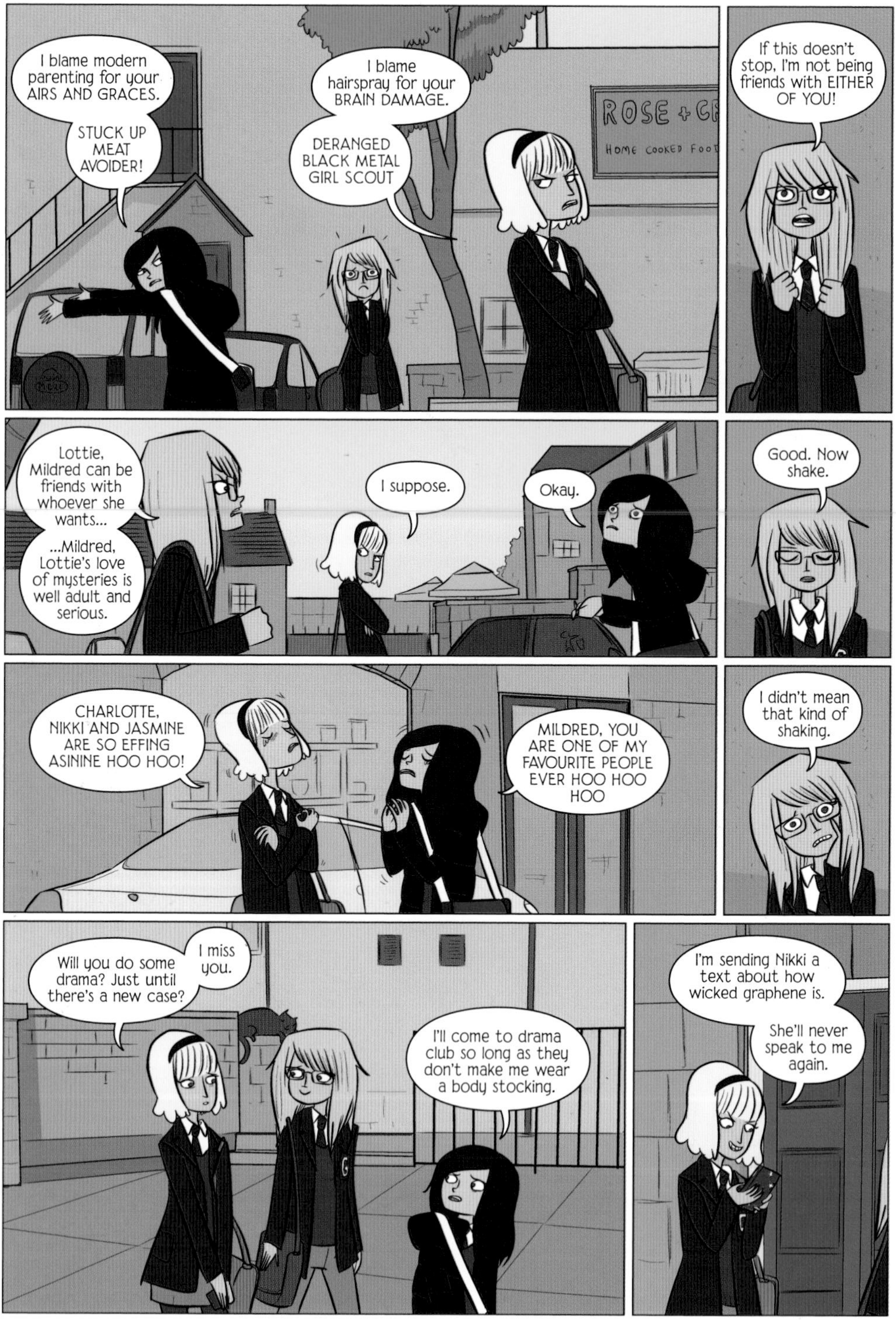
I blame modern parenting for your AIRS AND GRACES.
STUCK UP MEAT AVOIDER!
I blame hairspray for your BRAIN DAMAGE.
DERANGED BLACK METAL GIRL SCOUT
ROSE + CR
HOME COOKED FOO
If this doesn't stop, I'm not being friends with EITHER OF YOU!
Lottie, Mildred can be friends with whoever she wants...
...Mildred, Lottie's love of mysteries is well adult and serious.
I suppose.
Okay.
Good. Now shake.
CHARLOTTE, NIKKI AND JASMINE ARE SO EFFING ASININE HOO HOO!
MILDRED, YOU ARE ONE OF MY FAVOURITE PEOPLE EVER HOO HOO HOO
I didn't mean that kind of shaking.
Will you do some drama? Just until there's a new case?
I miss you.
I'll come to drama club so long as they don't make me wear a body stocking.
I'm sending Nikki a text about how wicked graphene is.
She'll never speak to me again.

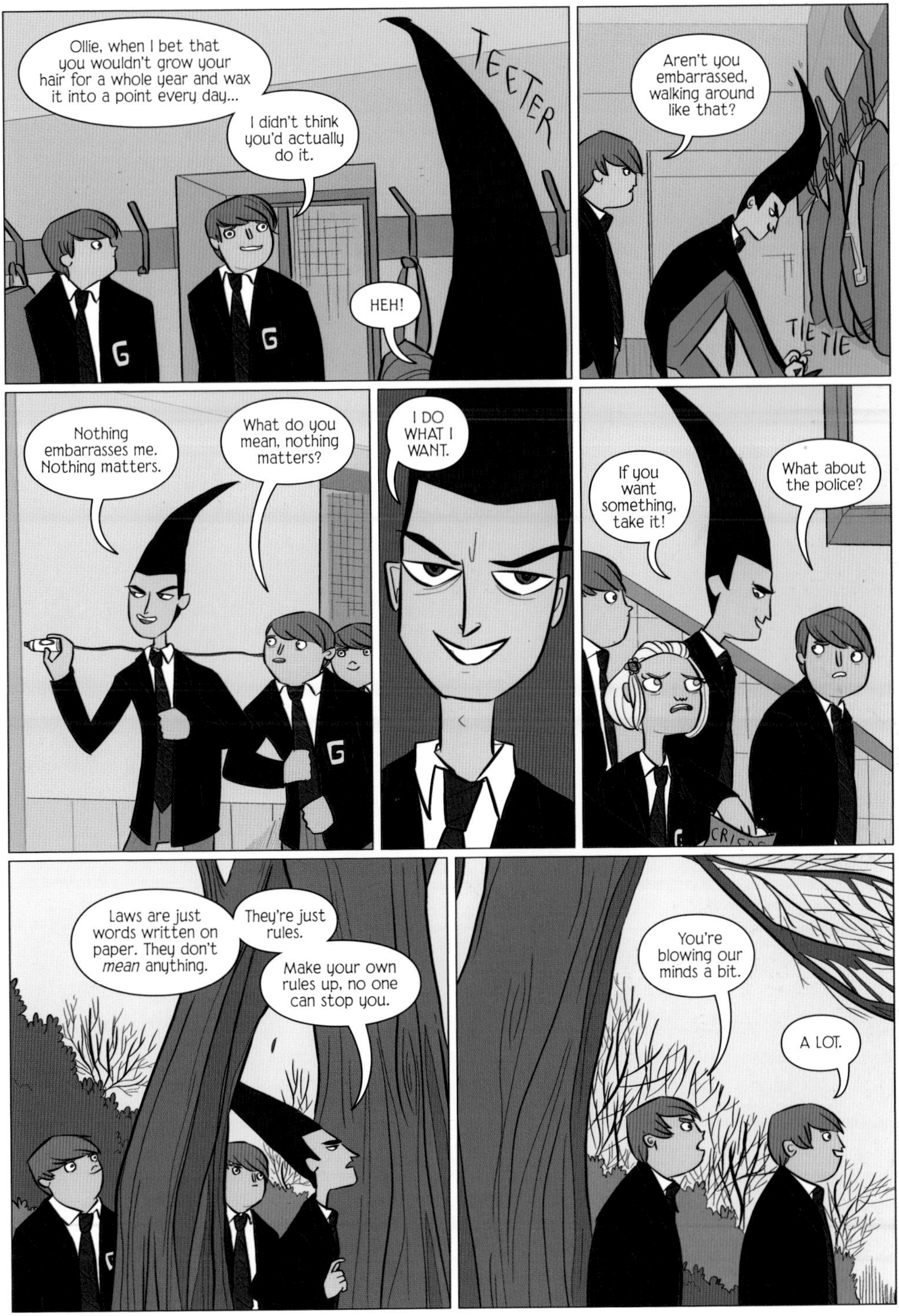
Ollie, when I bet that you wouldn't grow your hair for a whole year and wax it into a point every day...
I didn't think you'd actually do it.
TEETER
HEH!
Aren't you embarrassed, walking around like that?
TIE TIE
Nothing embarrasses me. Nothing matters.
What do you mean, nothing matters?
I DO WHAT I WANT.
If you want something, take it!
What about the police?
Laws are just words written on paper. They don't *mean* anything.
They're just rules.
Make your own rules up, no one can stop you.
You're blowing our minds a bit.
A LOT.

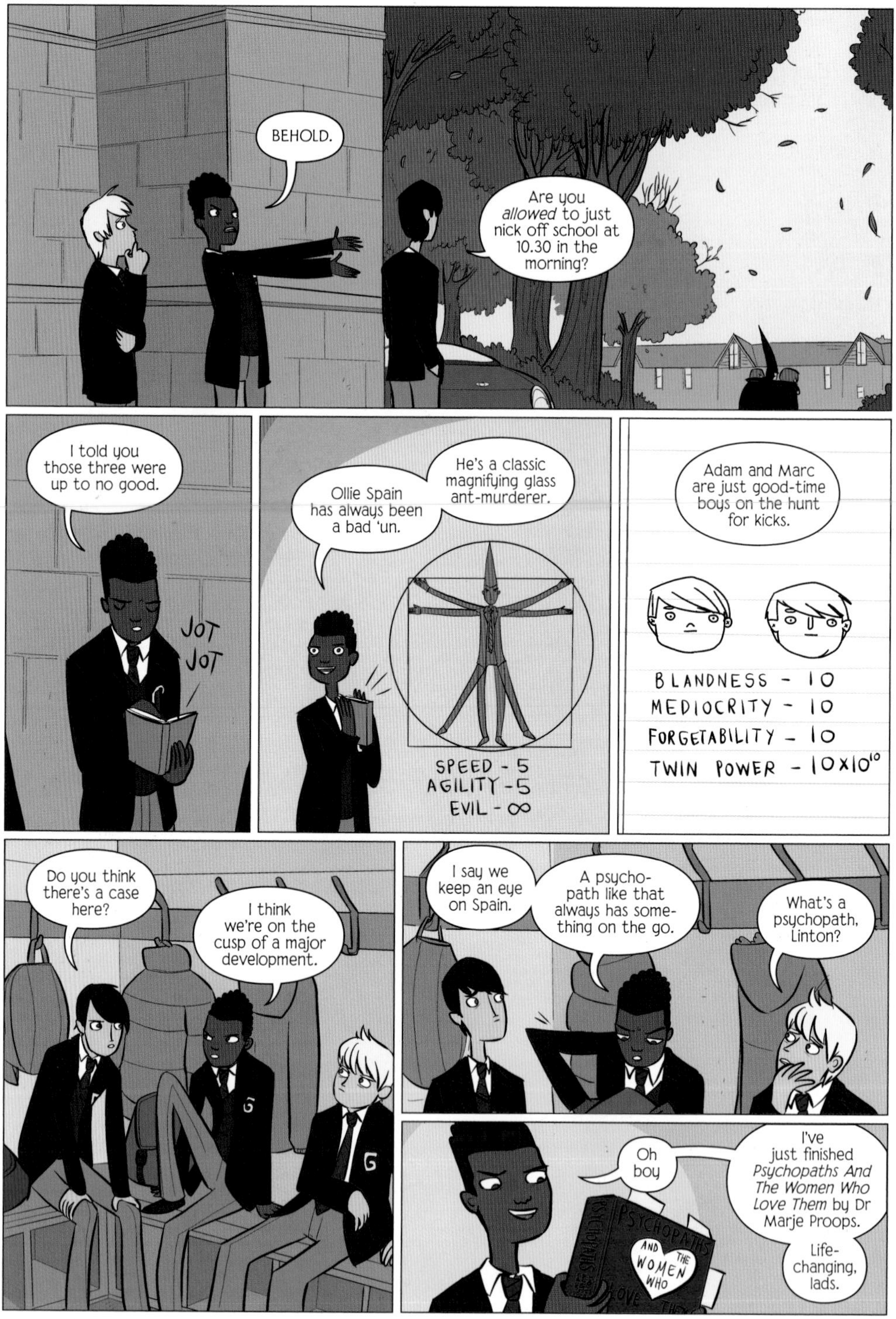
BEHOLD.
Are you *allowed* to just nick off school at 10.30 in the morning?
I told you those three were up to no good.
JOT JOT
Ollie Spain has always been a bad 'un.
He's a classic magnifying glass ant-murderer.
SPEED - 5
AGILITY - 5
EVIL - ∞
Adam and Marc are just good-time boys on the hunt for kicks.
BLANDNESS - 10
MEDIOCRITY - 10
FORGETABILITY - 10
TWIN POWER - 10x10[10]
Do you think there's a case here?
I think we're on the cusp of a major development.
I say we keep an eye on Spain.
A psychopath like that always has something on the go.
What's a psychopath, Linton?
Oh boy
I've just finished *Psychopaths And The Women Who Love Them* by Dr Marje Proops.
Life-changing, lads.
PSYCHOPATHS AND THE WOMEN WHO LOVE

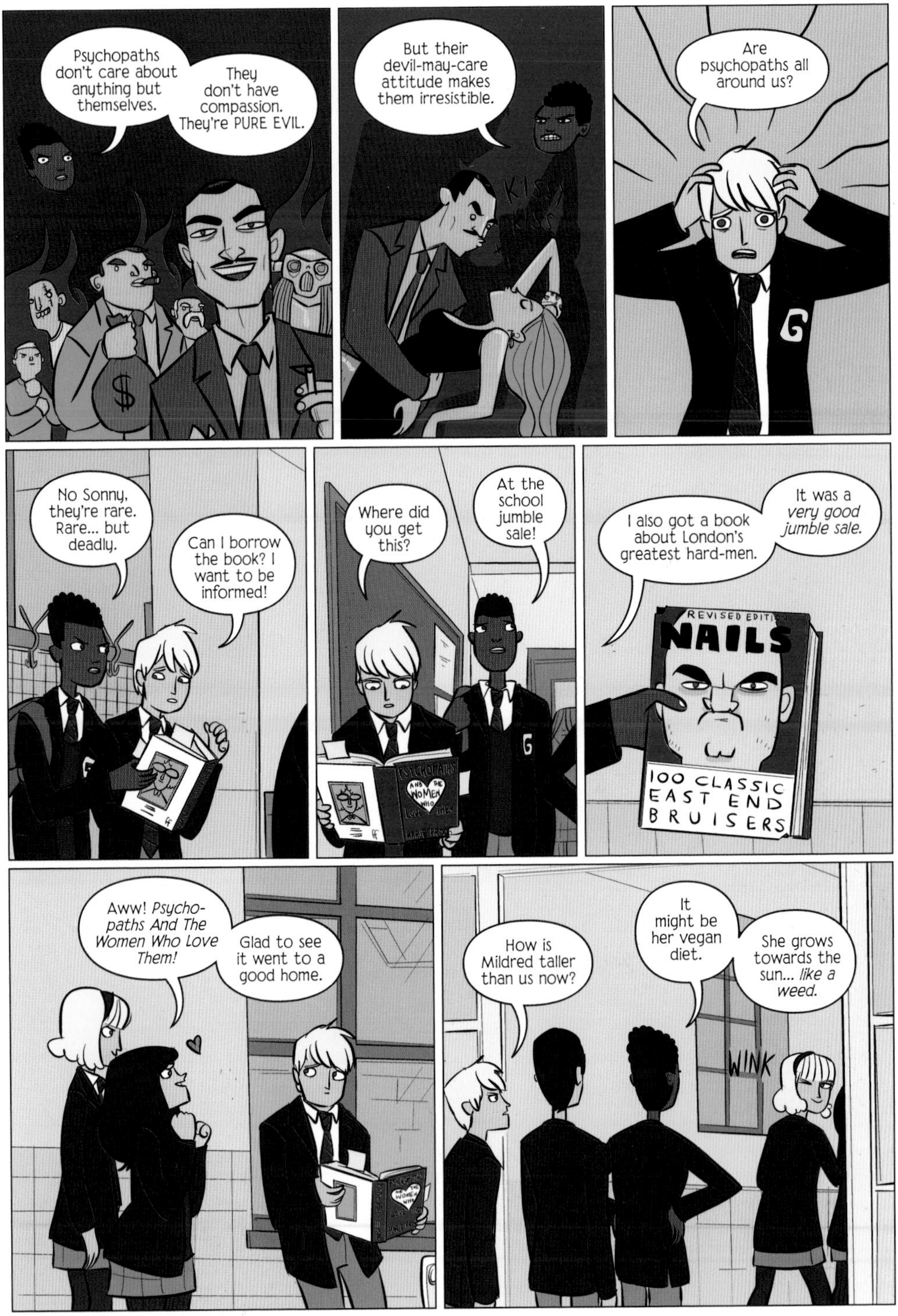
Psychopaths don't care about anything but themselves.
They don't have compassion. They're PURE EVIL.
But their devil-may-care attitude makes them irresistible.
KISS KISS
Are psychopaths all around us?
No Sonny, they're rare. Rare... but deadly.
Can I borrow the book? I want to be informed!
Where did you get this?
At the school jumble sale!
I also got a book about London's greatest hard-men.
It was a *very good jumble sale.*
REVISED EDITION
NAILS
100 CLASSIC EAST END BRUISERS
Aww! *Psychopaths And The Women Who Love Them!*
Glad to see it went to a good home.
How is Mildred taller than us now?
It might be her vegan diet.
She grows towards the sun... *like a weed.*
WINK

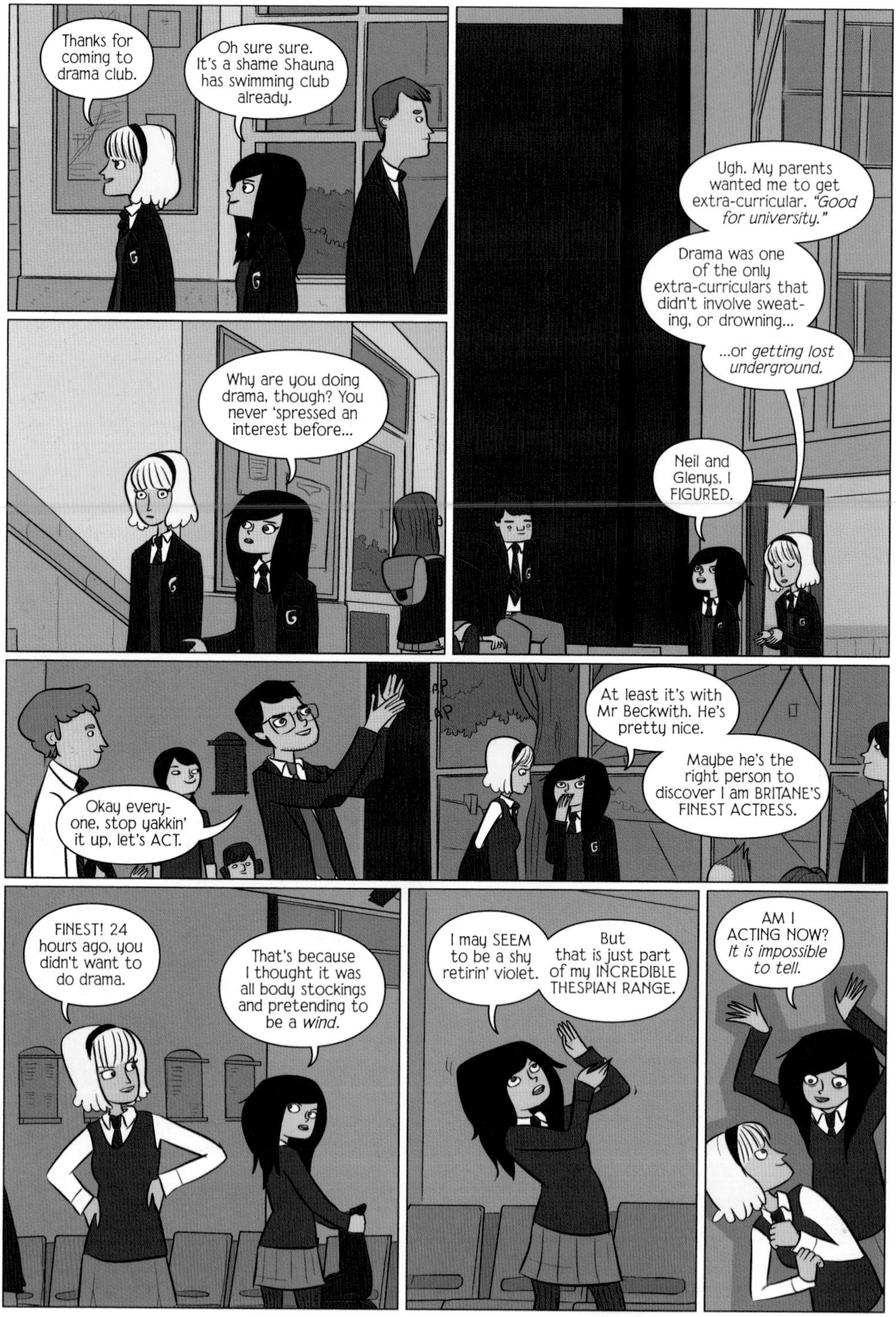
Thanks for coming to drama club.
Oh sure sure. It's a shame Shauna has swimming club already.
Why are you doing drama, though? You never 'spressed an interest before...
Ugh. My parents wanted me to get extra-curricular. *"Good for university."*
Drama was one of the only extra-curriculars that didn't involve sweat- ing, or drowning...
...or *getting lost underground.*
Neil and Glenys, I FIGURED.
Okay every- one, stop yakkin' it up, let's ACT.
At least it's with Mr Beckwith. He's pretty nice.
Maybe he's the right person to discover I am BRITANE'S FINEST ACTRESS.
FINEST! 24 hours ago, you didn't want to do drama.
That's because I thought it was all body stockings and pretending to be a *wind.*
I may SEEM to be a shy retirin' violet.
But that is just part of my INCREDIBLE THESPIAN RANGE.
AM I ACTING NOW? *It is impossible to tell.*

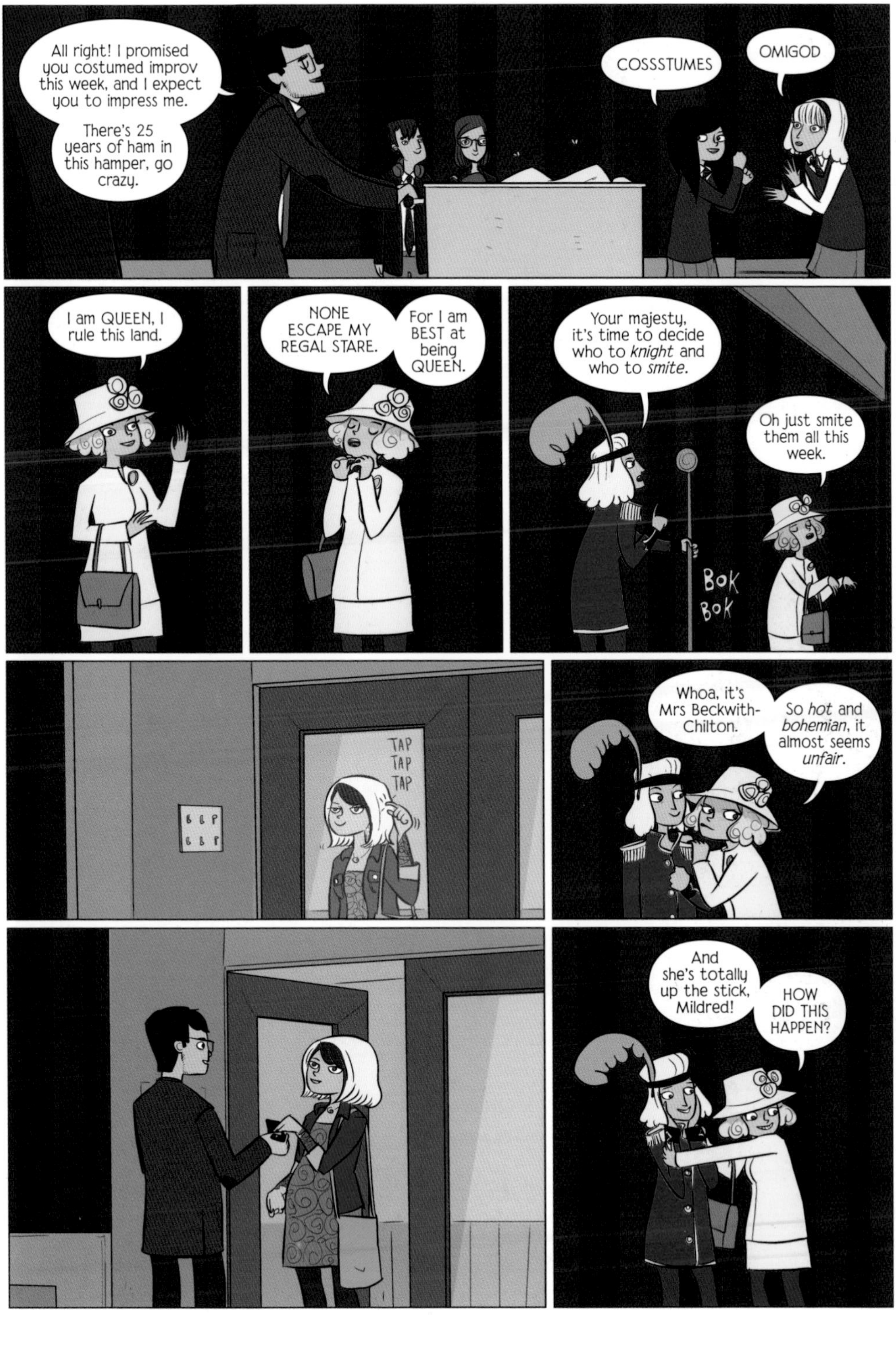
All right! I promised you costumed improv this week, and I expect you to impress me.
There's 25 years of ham in this hamper, go crazy.
COSSSTUMES
OMIGOD
I am QUEEN, I rule this land.
NONE ESCAPE MY REGAL STARE.
For I am BEST at being QUEEN.
Your majesty, it's time to decide who to *knight* and who to *smite*.
Oh just smite them all this week.
BOK
BOK
TAP
TAP
TAP
Whoa, it's Mrs Beckwith-Chilton.
So *hot* and *bohemian*, it almost seems *unfair*.
And she's totally up the stick, Mildred!
HOW DID THIS HAPPEN?

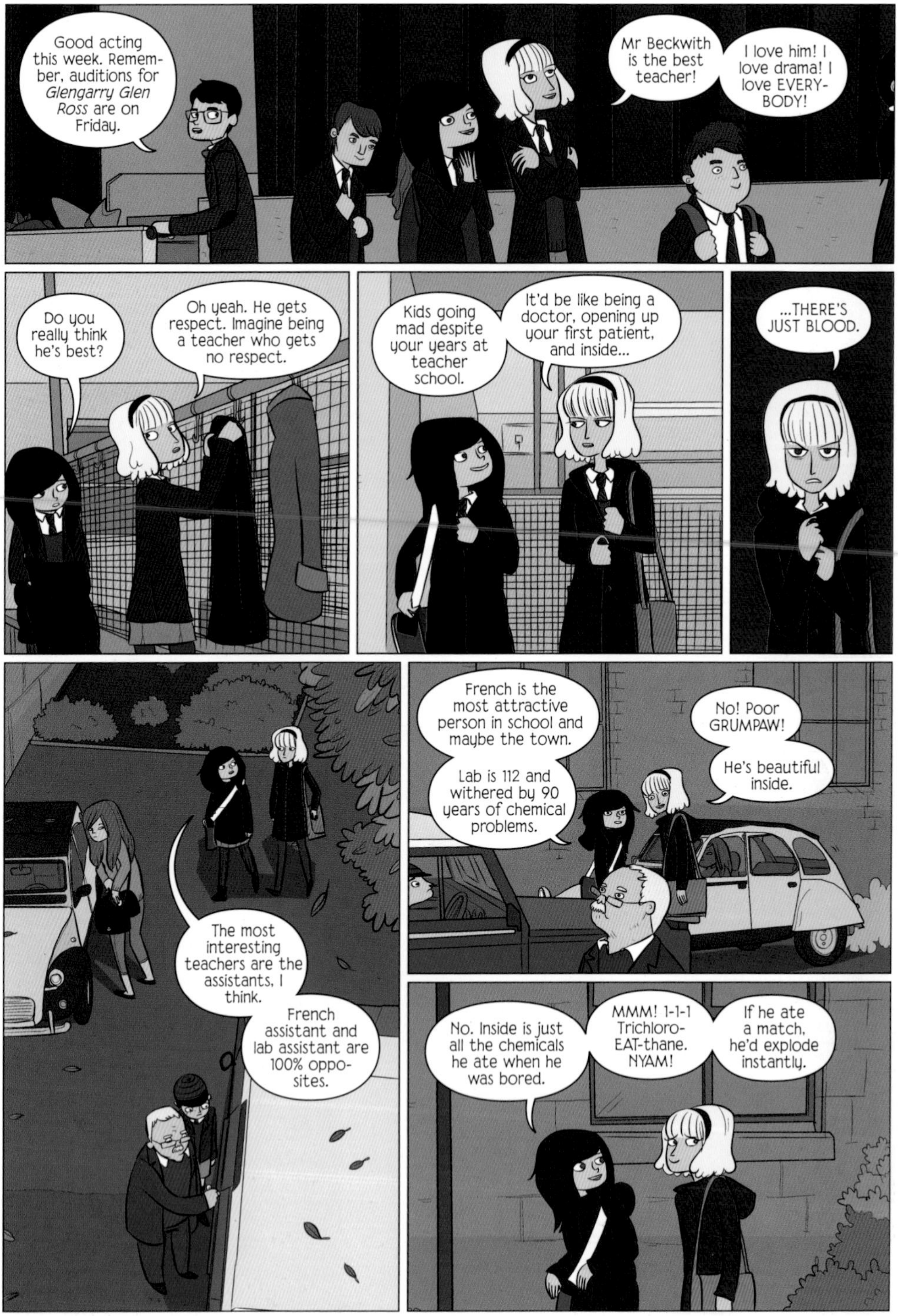
Good acting this week. Remember, auditions for *Glengarry Glen Ross* are on Friday.
Mr Beckwith is the best teacher!
I love him! I love drama! I love EVERYBODY!
Do you really think he's best?
Oh yeah. He gets respect. Imagine being a teacher who gets no respect.
Kids going mad despite your years at teacher school.
It'd be like being a doctor, opening up your first patient, and inside...
...THERE'S JUST BLOOD.
The most interesting teachers are the assistants, I think.
French assistant and lab assistant are 100% opposites.
French is the most attractive person in school and maybe the town.
Lab is 112 and withered by 90 years of chemical problems.
No! Poor GRUMPAW!
He's beautiful inside.
No. Inside is just all the chemicals he ate when he was bored.
MMM! 1-1-1 Trichloro-EAT-thane. NYAM!
If he ate a match, he'd explode instantly.

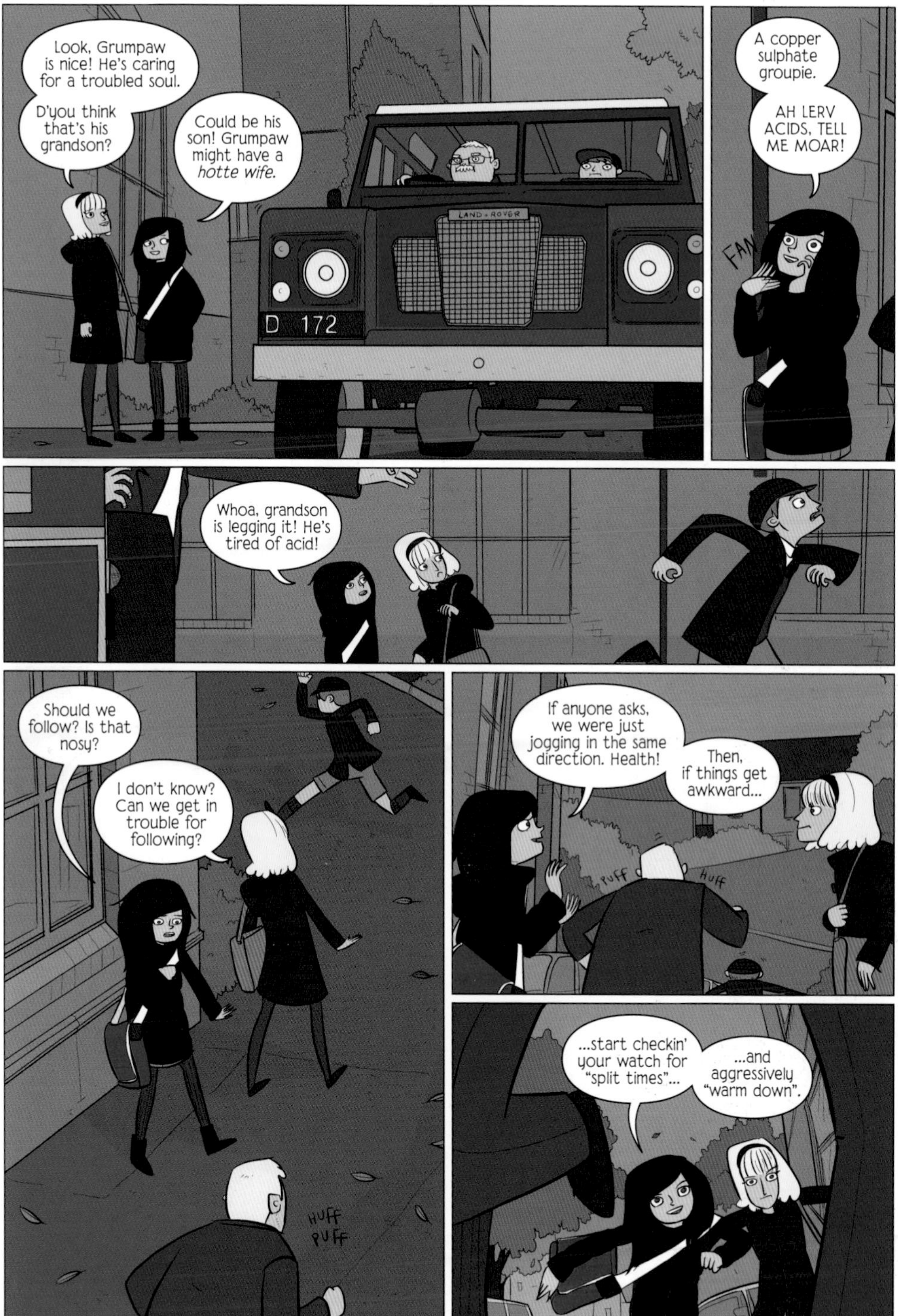
Look, Grumpaw is nice! He's caring for a troubled soul.
D'you think that's his grandson?
Could be his son! Grumpaw might have a *hotte wife.*
LAND ROVER
D 172
A copper sulphate groupie.
AH LERV ACIDS, TELL ME MOAR!
FAN
Whoa, grandson is legging it! He's tired of acid!
Should we follow? Is that nosy?
I don't know? Can we get in trouble for following?
HUFF PUFF
If anyone asks, we were just jogging in the same direction. Health!
Then, if things get awkward...
PUFF
HUFF
...start checkin' your watch for "split times"...
...and aggressively "warm down".

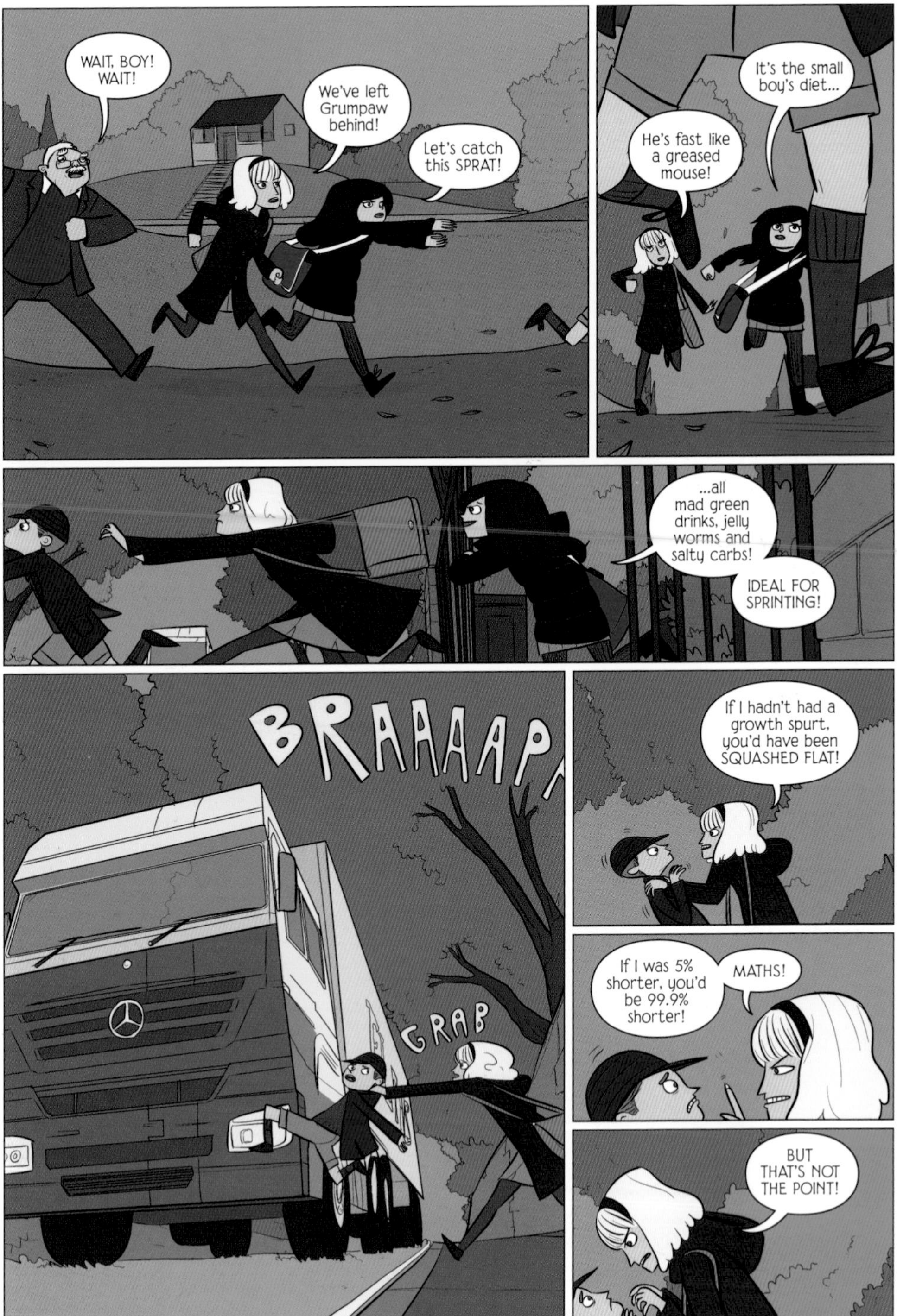
WAIT, BOY!
WAIT!
We've left Grumpaw behind!
Let's catch this SPRAT!
It's the small boy's diet...
He's fast like a greased mouse!
...all mad green drinks, jelly worms and salty carbs!
IDEAL FOR SPRINTING!
BRAAAAP
GRAB
If I hadn't had a growth spurt, you'd have been SQUASHED FLAT!
If I was 5% shorter, you'd be 99.9% shorter!
MATHS!
BUT THAT'S NOT THE POINT!

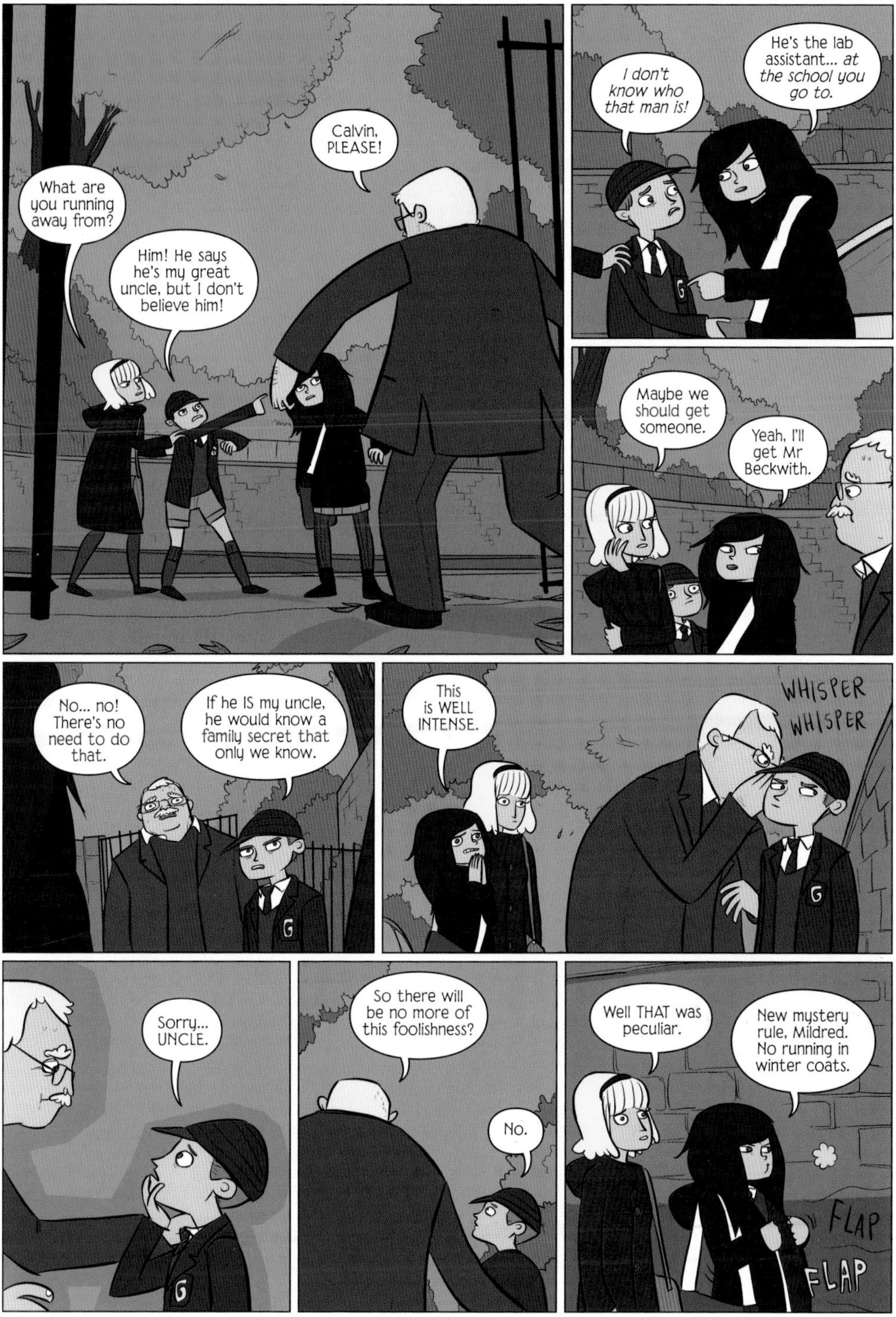
Calvin, PLEASE!
What are you running away from?
Him! He says he's my great uncle, but I don't believe him!
I don't know who that man is!
He's the lab assistant... at the school you go to.
Maybe we should get someone.
Yeah, I'll get Mr Beckwith.
No... no! There's no need to do that.
If he IS my uncle, he would know a family secret that only we know.
This is WELL INTENSE.
WHISPER WHISPER
Sorry... UNCLE.
So there will be no more of this foolishness?
No.
Well THAT was peculiar.
New mystery rule, Mildred. No running in winter coats.
FLAP
FLAP

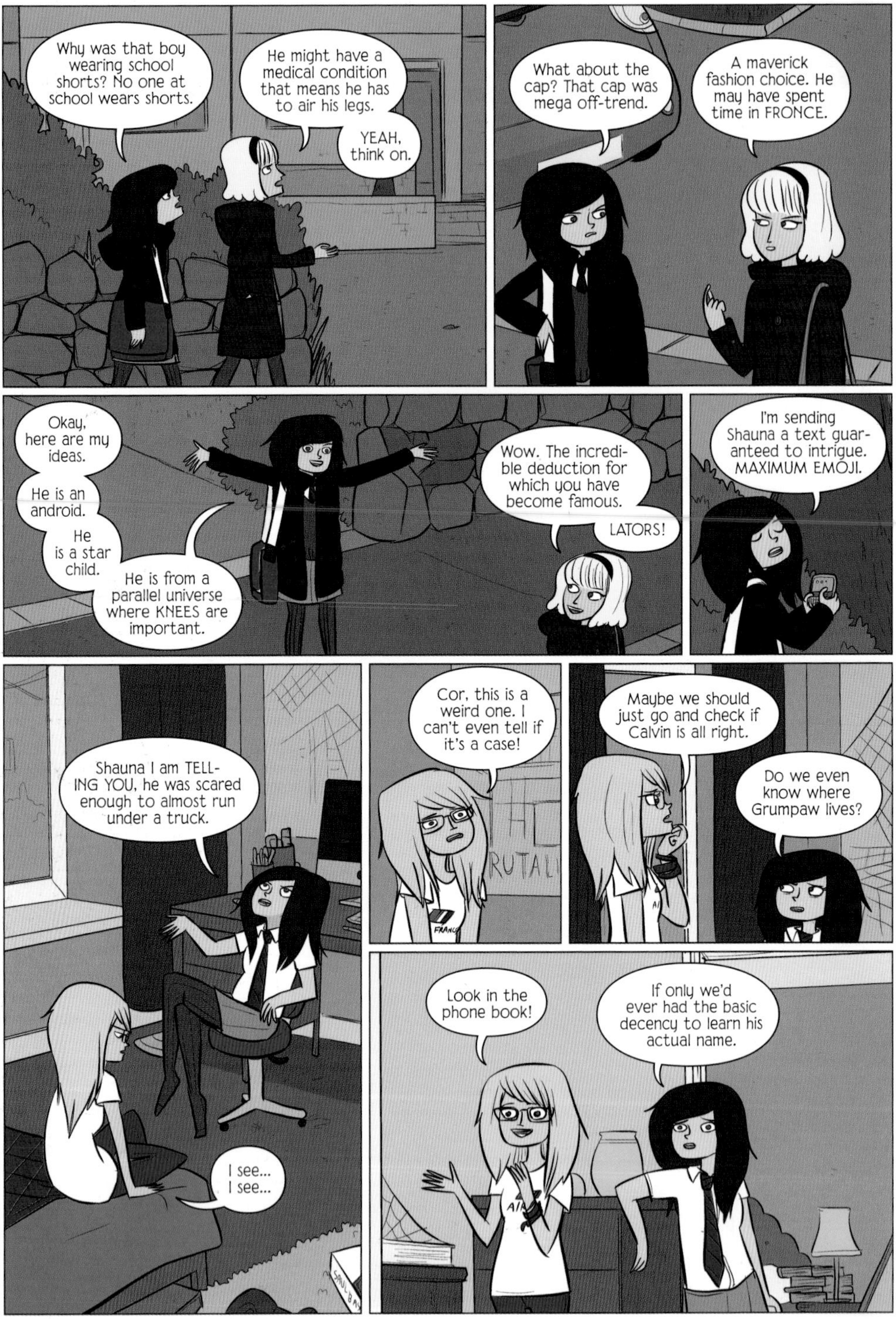
Why was that boy wearing school shorts? No one at school wears shorts.
He might have a medical condition that means he has to air his legs.
YEAH, think on.
What about the cap? That cap was mega off-trend.
A maverick fashion choice. He may have spent time in FRONCE.
Okay, here are my ideas.
He is an android.
He is a star child.
He is from a parallel universe where KNEES are important.
Wow. The incredible deduction for which you have become famous.
LATORS!
I'm sending Shauna a text guaranteed to intrigue. MAXIMUM EMOJI.
Shauna I am TELLING YOU, he was scared enough to almost run under a truck.
I see... I see...
Cor, this is a weird one. I can't even tell if it's a case!
Maybe we should just go and check if Calvin is all right.
Do we even know where Grumpaw lives?
Look in the phone book!
If only we'd ever had the basic decency to learn his actual name.

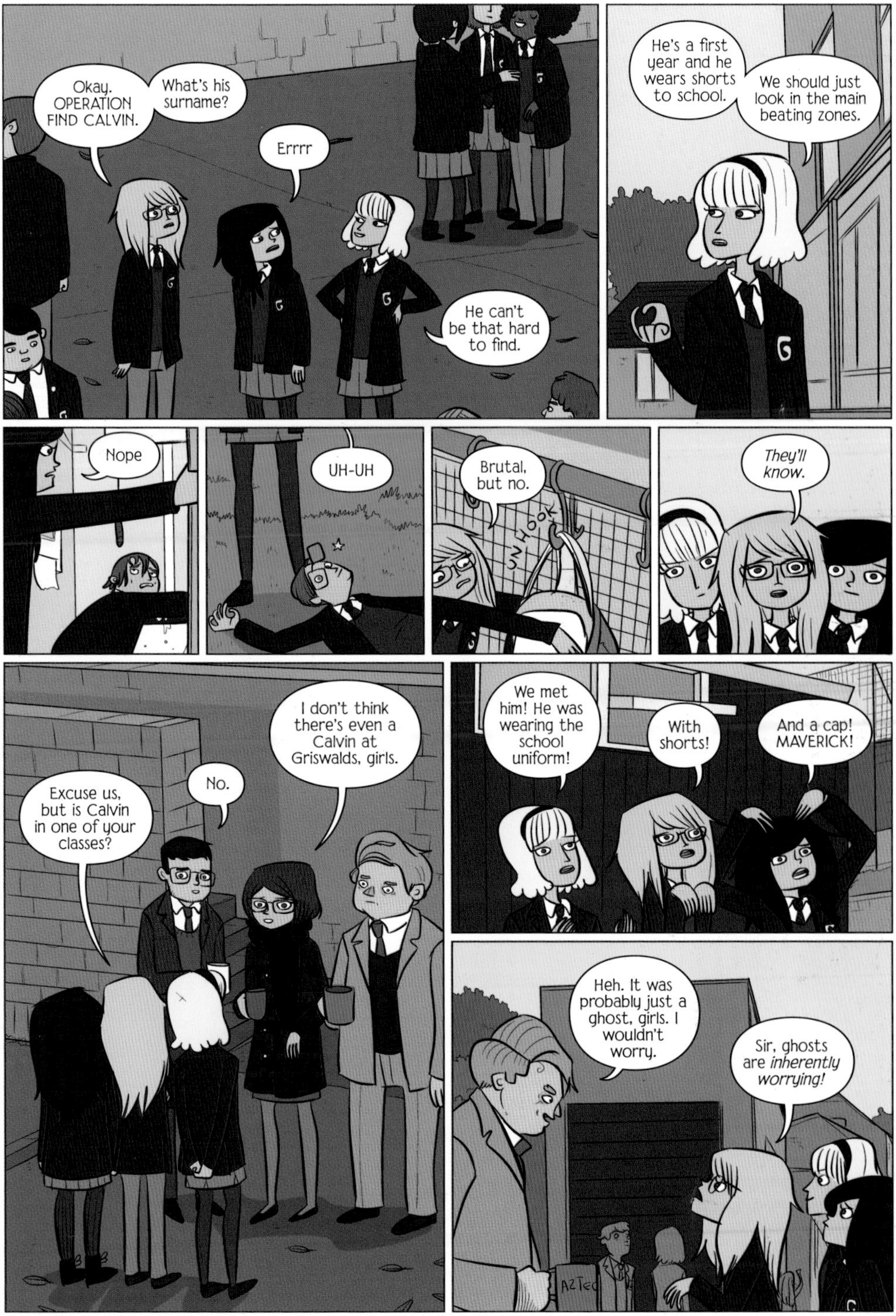
Okay. OPERATION FIND CALVIN.
What's his surname?
Errrr
He can't be that hard to find.
He's a first year and he wears shorts to school.
We should just look in the main beating zones.
Nope
UH-UH
Brutal, but no.
UNHOOK
They'll know.
Excuse us, but is Calvin in one of your classes?
No.
I don't think there's even a Calvin at Griswalds, girls.
We met him! He was wearing the school uniform!
With shorts!
And a cap! MAVERICK!
Heh. It was probably just a ghost, girls. I wouldn't worry.
Sir, ghosts are *inherently worrying!*

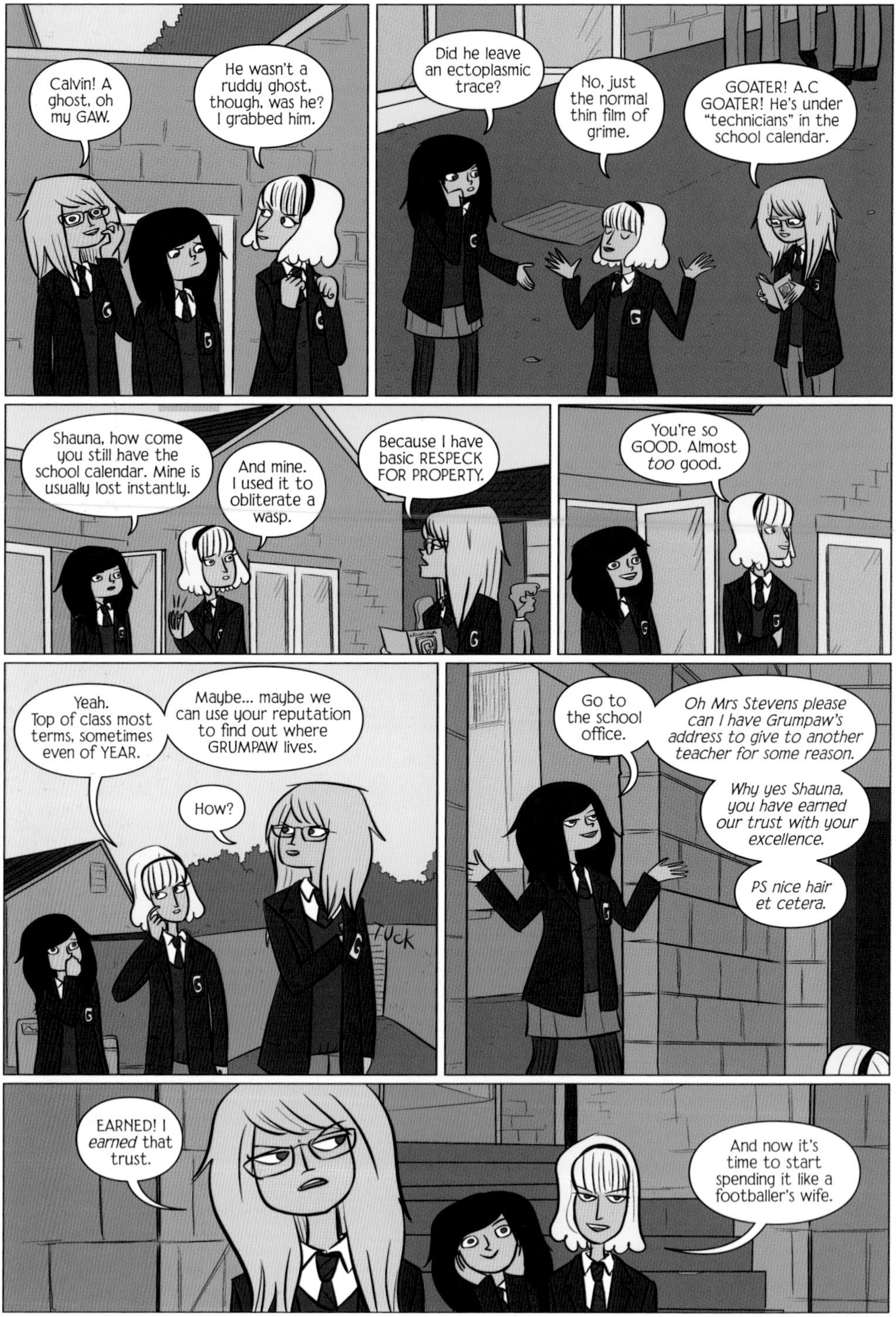
Calvin! A ghost, oh my GAW.
He wasn't a ruddy ghost, though, was he? I grabbed him.
Did he leave an ectoplasmic trace?
No, just the normal thin film of grime.
GOATER! A.C GOATER! He's under "technicians" in the school calendar.
Shauna, how come you still have the school calendar. Mine is usually lost instantly.
And mine. I used it to obliterate a wasp.
Because I have basic RESPECK FOR PROPERTY.
You're so GOOD. Almost *too* good.
Yeah. Top of class most terms, sometimes even of YEAR.
Maybe... maybe we can use your reputation to find out where GRUMPAW lives.
How?
Go to the school office.
Oh Mrs Stevens please can I have Grumpaw's address to give to another teacher for some reason.
Why yes Shauna, you have earned our trust with your excellence.
PS nice hair et cetera.
EARNED! I *earned* that trust.
And now it's time to start spending it like a footballer's wife.

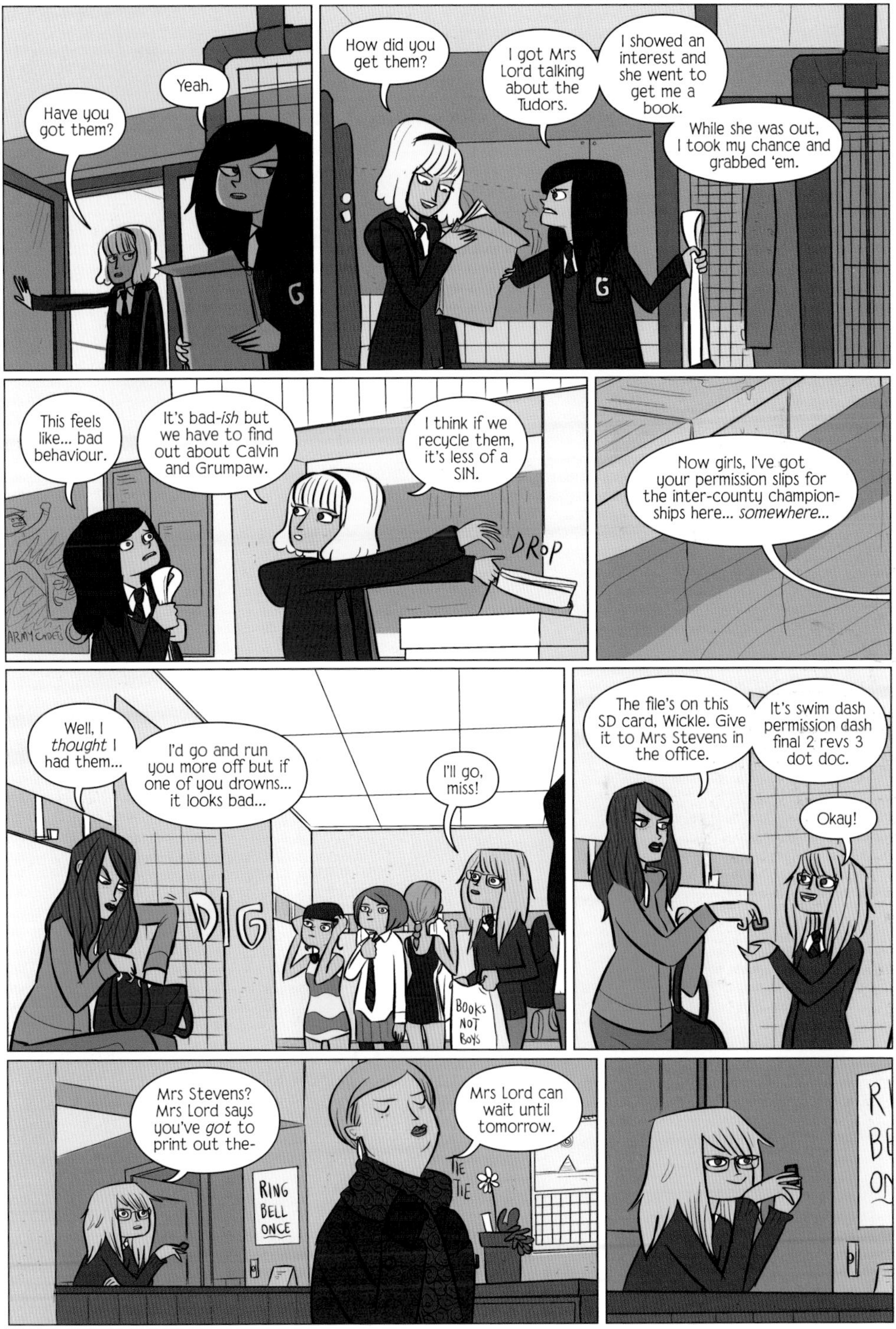

Have you got them?
Yeah.
How did you get them?
I got Mrs Lord talking about the Tudors.
I showed an interest and she went to get me a book.
While she was out, I took my chance and grabbed 'em.
This feels like... bad behaviour.
It's bad-*ish* but we have to find out about Calvin and Grumpaw.
I think if we recycle them, it's less of a SIN.
DROP
ARMY CADETS
Now girls, I've got your permission slips for the inter-county championships here... *somewhere*...
Well, I *thought* I had them...
I'd go and run you more off but if one of you drowns... it looks bad...
I'll go, miss!
DIG
BOOKS NOT BOYS
The file's on this SD card, Wickle. Give it to Mrs Stevens in the office.
It's swim dash permission dash final 2 revs 3 dot doc.
Okay!
Mrs Stevens? Mrs Lord says you've *got* to print out the-
Mrs Lord can wait until tomorrow.
RING BELL ONCE
TIE TIE

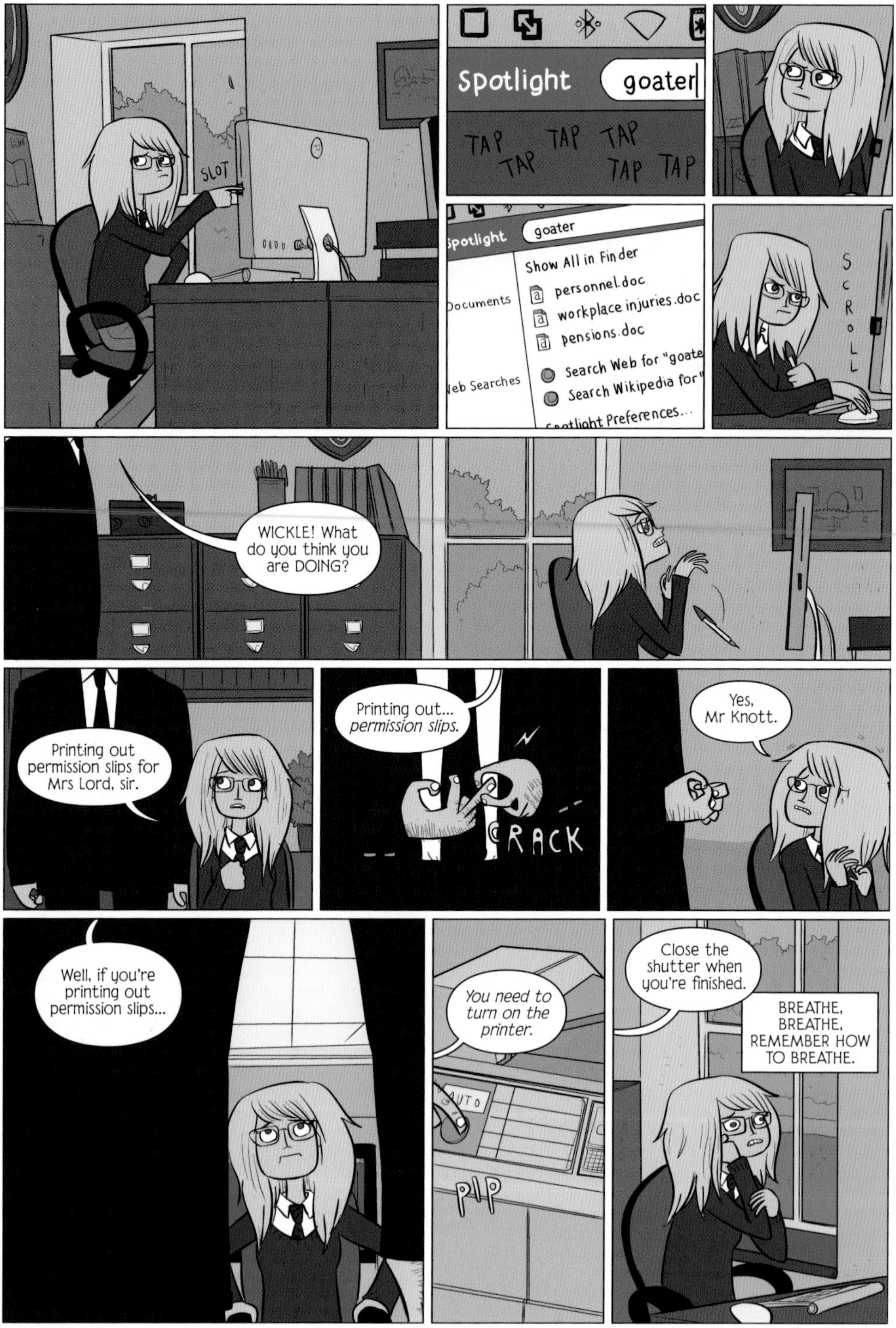
SLOT
Spotlight
goater
TAP TAP TAP TAP TAP TAP TAP
Spotlight
goater
Show All in Finder
Documents
personnel.doc
workplace injuries.doc
pensions.doc
Web Searches
Search Web for "goate
Search Wikipedia for"
Spotlight Preferences...
SCROLL
WICKLE! What do you think you are DOING?
Printing out permission slips for Mrs Lord, sir.
Printing out... *permission slips.*
CRACK
Yes, Mr Knott.
Well, if you're printing out permission slips...
You need to turn on the printer.
AUTO
PIP
Close the shutter when you're finished.
BREATHE, BREATHE, REMEMBER HOW TO BREATHE.

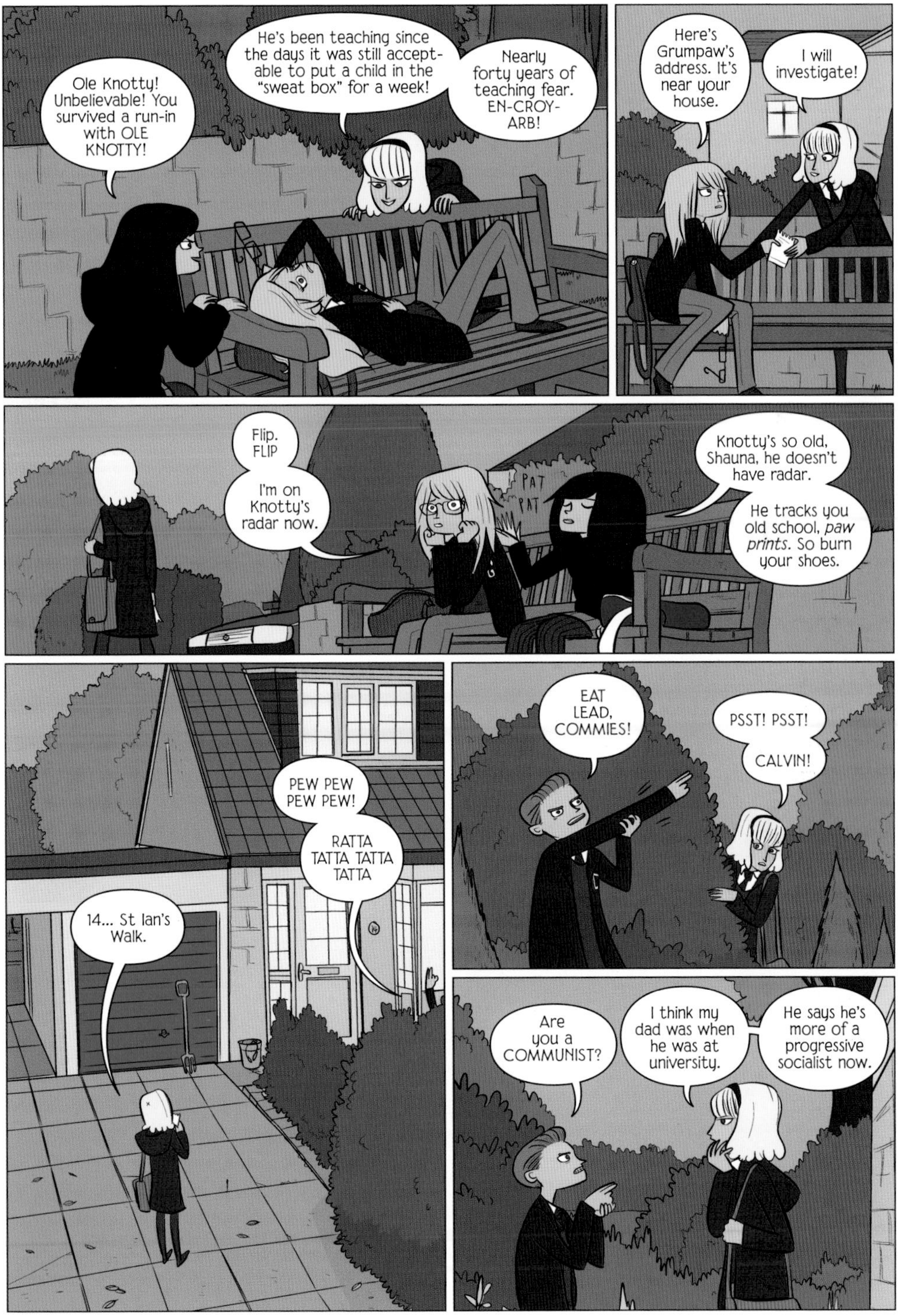
Ole Knotty! Unbelievable! You survived a run-in with OLE KNOTTY!
He's been teaching since the days it was still acceptable to put a child in the "sweat box" for a week!
Nearly forty years of teaching fear. EN-CROY-ARB!
Here's Grumpaw's address. It's near your house.
I will investigate!
Flip. FLIP
I'm on Knotty's radar now.
PAT PAT
Knotty's so old, Shauna, he doesn't have radar.
He tracks you old school, *paw prints*. So burn your shoes.
PEW PEW PEW PEW!
RATTA TATTA TATTA TATTA
14... St Ian's Walk.
EAT LEAD, COMMIES!
PSST! PSST!
CALVIN!
Are you a COMMUNIST?
I think my dad was when he was at university.
He says he's more of a progressive socialist now.

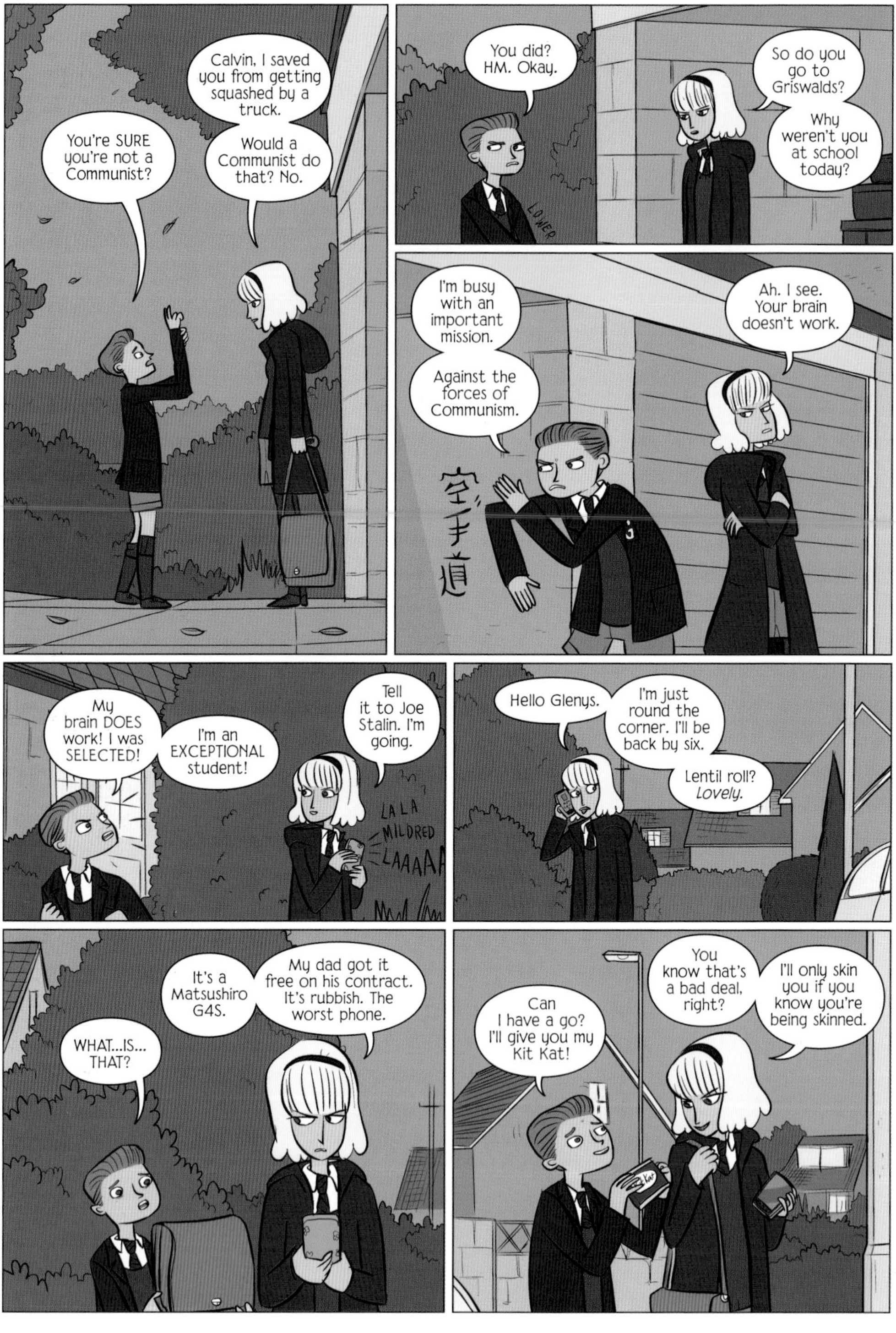
You're SURE you're not a Communist?
Calvin, I saved you from getting squashed by a truck.
Would a Communist do that? No.
You did? HM. Okay.
LOWER
So do you go to Griswalds?
Why weren't you at school today?
I'm busy with an important mission.
Against the forces of Communism.
Ah. I see. Your brain doesn't work.
空手道
My brain DOES work! I was SELECTED!
I'm an EXCEPTIONAL student!
Tell it to Joe Stalin. I'm going.
LA LA MILDRED LAAAAA
Hello Glenys.
I'm just round the corner. I'll be back by six.
Lentil roll? *Lovely.*
WHAT...IS... THAT?
It's a Matsushiro G4S.
My dad got it free on his contract. It's rubbish. The worst phone.
Can I have a go? I'll give you my Kit Kat!
You know that's a bad deal, right?
I'll only skin you if you know you're being skinned.

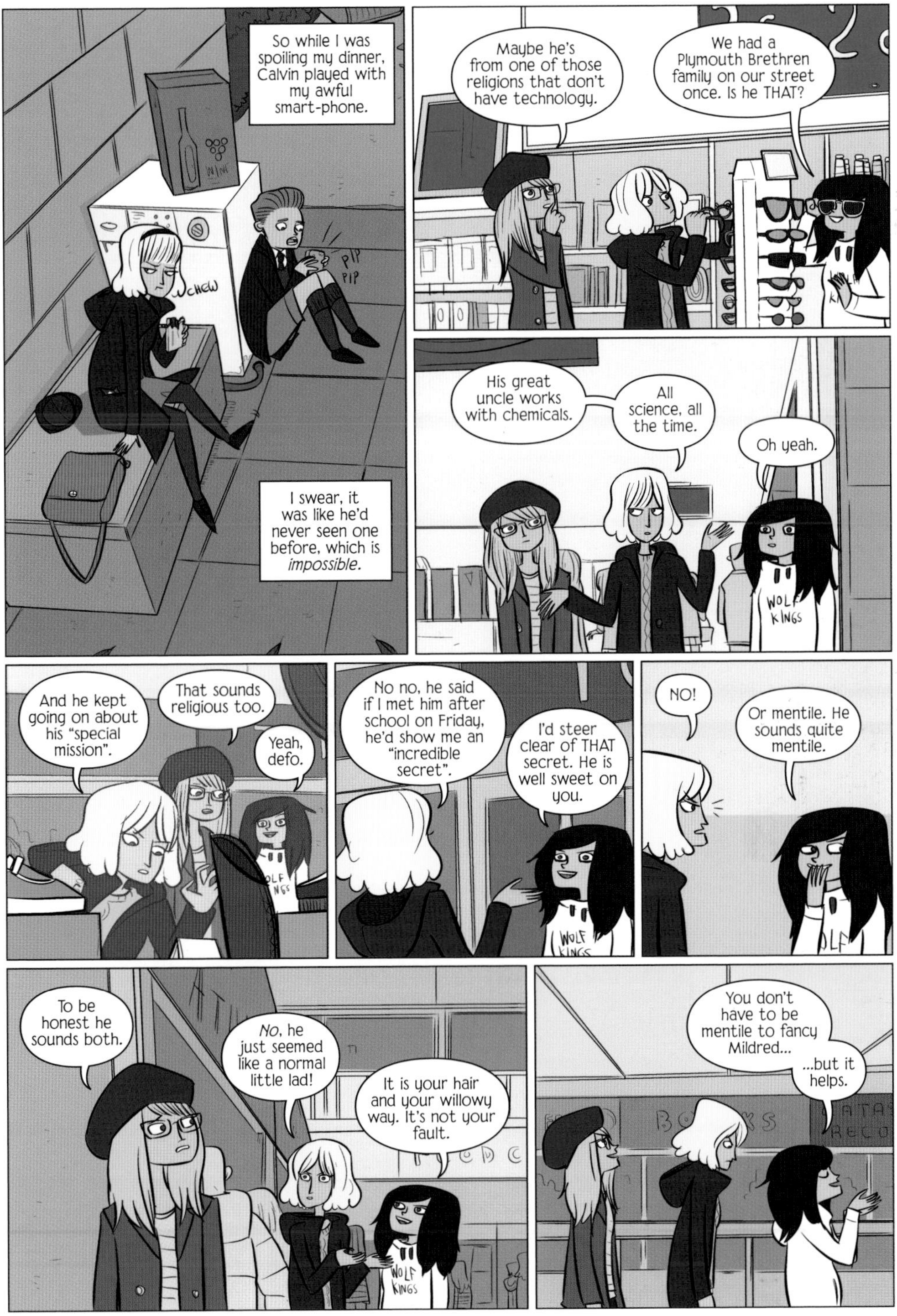
So while I was spoiling my dinner, Calvin played with my awful smart-phone.
CHEW
PIP PIP
I swear, it was like he'd never seen one before, which is *impossible*.
Maybe he's from one of those religions that don't have technology.
We had a Plymouth Brethren family on our street once. Is he THAT?
His great uncle works with chemicals.
All science, all the time.
Oh yeah.
WOLF KINGS
And he kept going on about his "special mission".
That sounds religious too.
Yeah, defo.
No no, he said if I met him after school on Friday, he'd show me an "incredible secret".
I'd steer clear of THAT secret. He is well sweet on you.
NO!
Or mentile. He sounds quite mentile.
To be honest he sounds both.
No, he just seemed like a normal little lad!
It is your hair and your willowy way. It's not your fault.
WOLF KINGS
You don't have to be mentile to fancy Mildred...
...but it helps.

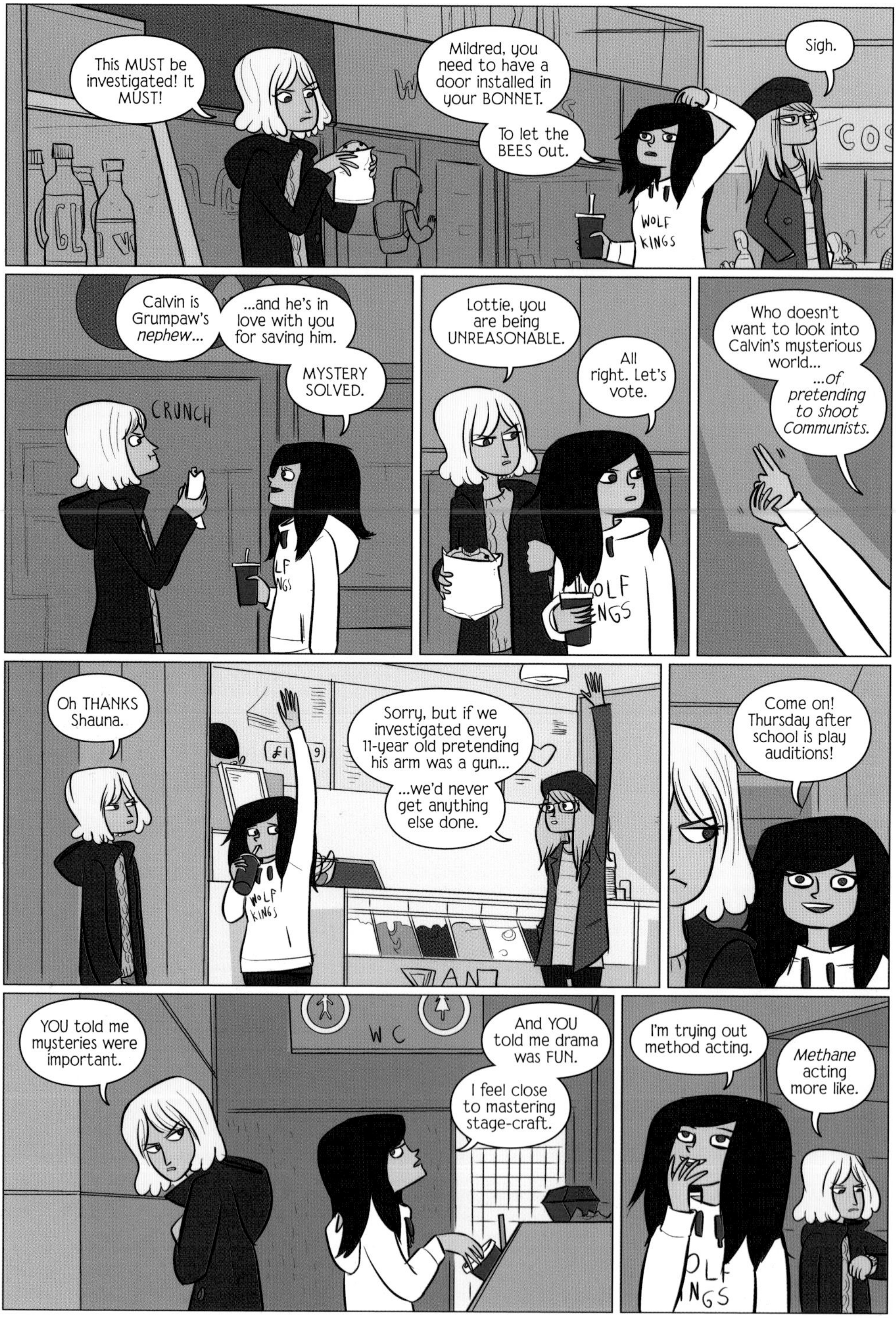
This MUST be investigated! It MUST!
Mildred, you need to have a door installed in your BONNET.
To let the BEES out.
Sigh.
WOLF KINGS
Calvin is Grumpaw's *nephew*...
...and he's in love with you for saving him.
MYSTERY SOLVED.
CRUNCH
Lottie, you are being UNREASONABLE.
All right. Let's vote.
Who doesn't want to look into Calvin's mysterious world...
...of pretending to shoot Communists.
Oh THANKS Shauna.
Sorry, but if we investigated every 11-year old pretending his arm was a gun...
...we'd never get anything else done.
Come on! Thursday after school is play auditions!
YOU told me mysteries were important.
And YOU told me drama was FUN.
I feel close to mastering stage-craft.
W C
I'm trying out method acting.
Methane acting more like.

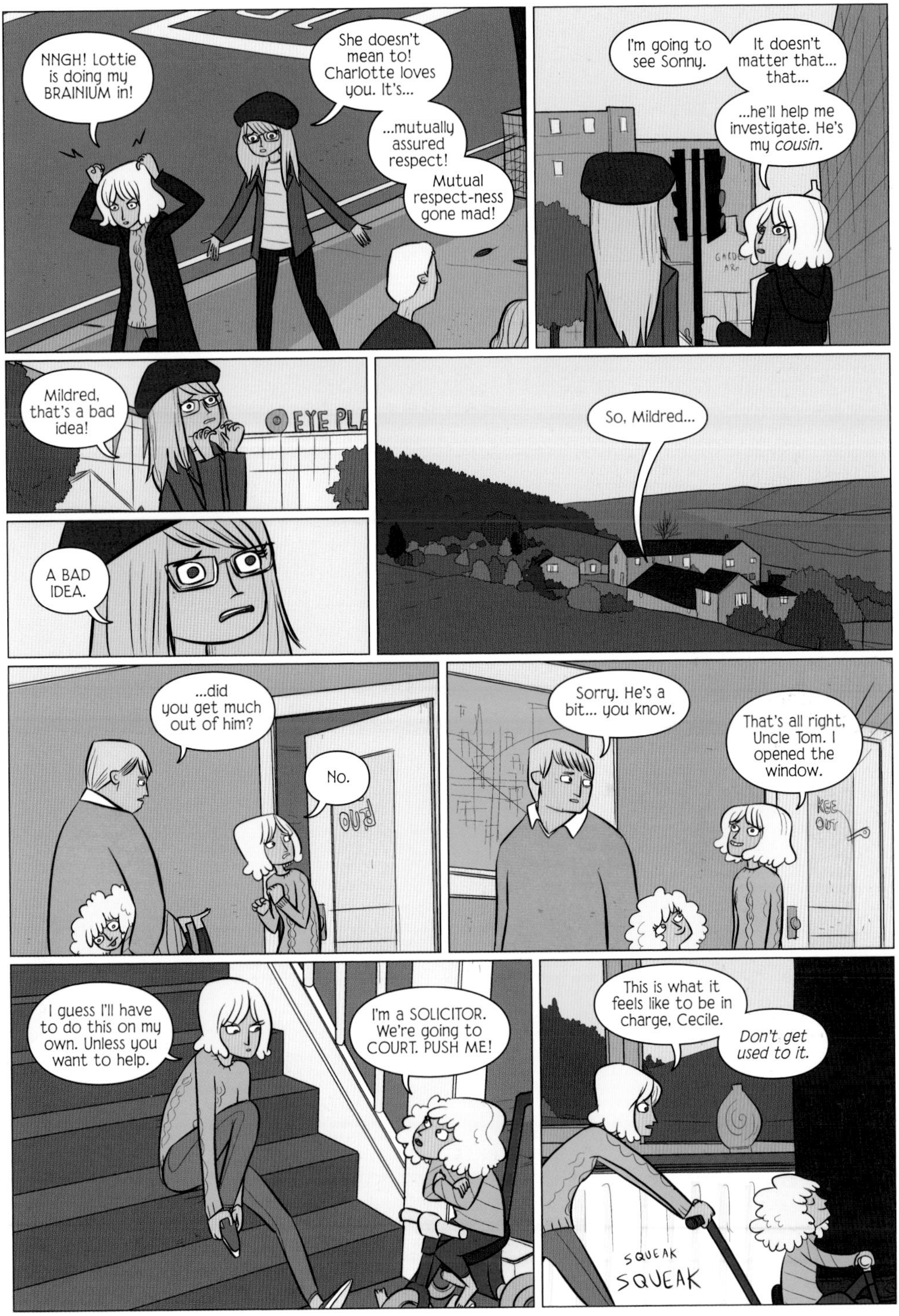
NNGH! Lottie is doing my BRAINIUM in!
She doesn't mean to! Charlotte loves you. It's...
...mutually assured respect!
Mutual respect-ness gone mad!
I'm going to see Sonny.
It doesn't matter that... that...
...he'll help me investigate. He's my *cousin*.
Mildred, that's a bad idea!
A BAD IDEA.
So, Mildred...
...did you get much out of him?
No.
Sorry. He's a bit... you know.
That's all right, Uncle Tom. I opened the window.
I guess I'll have to do this on my own. Unless you want to help.
I'm a SOLICITOR. We're going to COURT. PUSH ME!
This is what it feels like to be in charge, Cecile.
Don't get used to it.
SQUEAK
SQUEAK

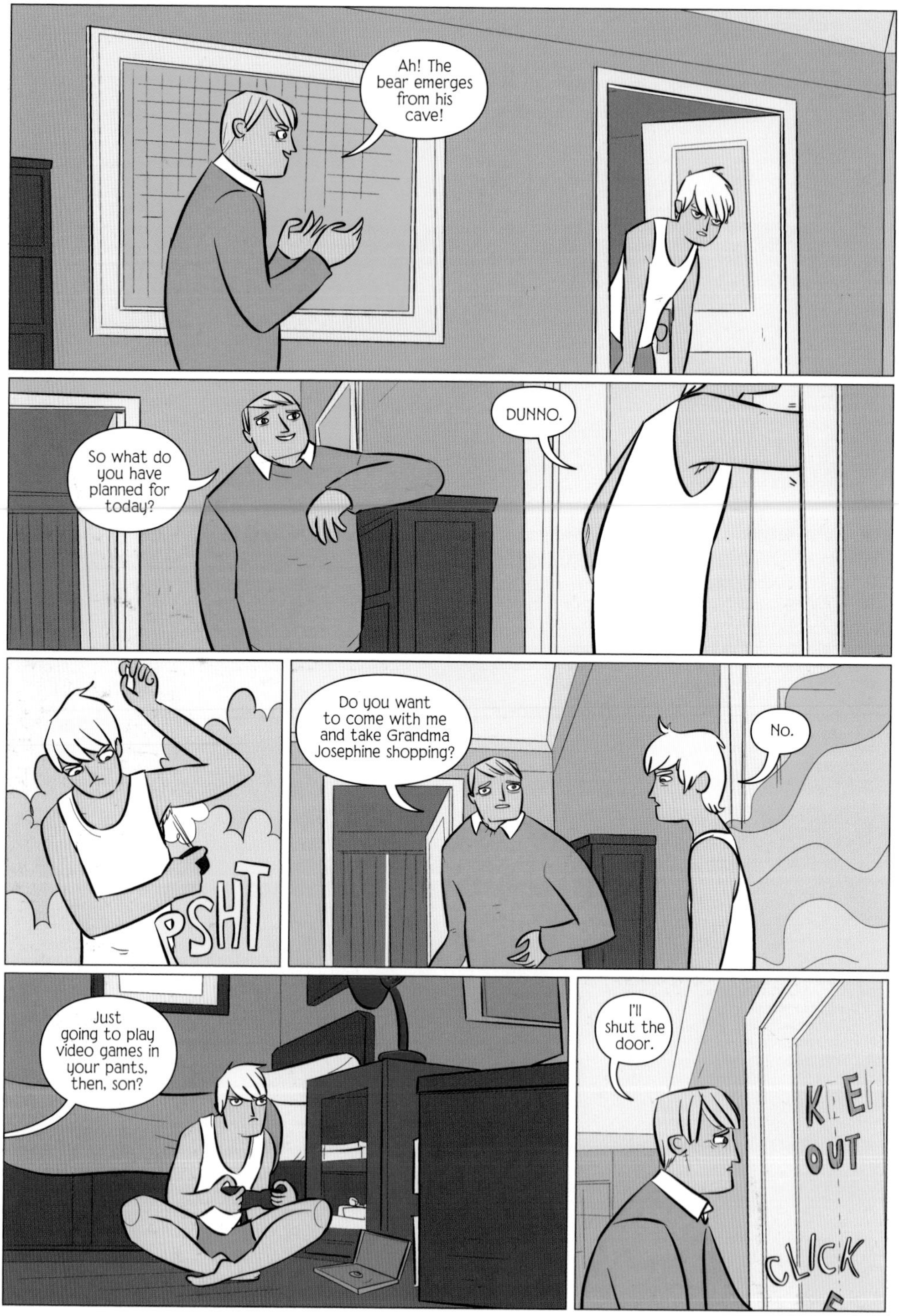
Ah! The bear emerges from his cave!
So what do you have planned for today?
DUNNO.
PSHT
Do you want to come with me and take Grandma Josephine shopping?
No.
Just going to play video games in your pants, then, son?
I'll shut the door.
KEEP OUT
CLICK

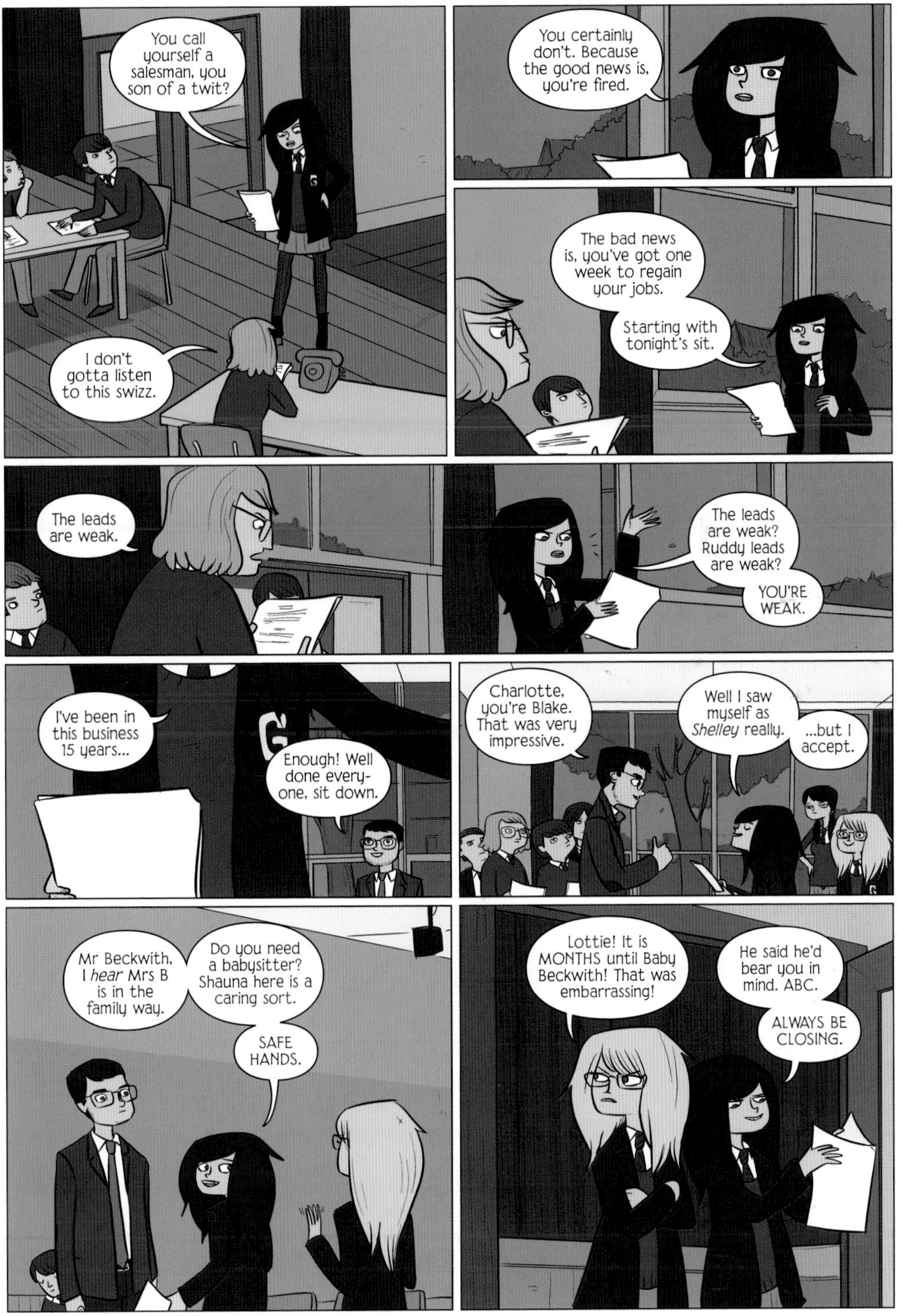
You call yourself a salesman, you son of a twit?
I don't gotta listen to this swizz.
You certainly don't. Because the good news is, you're fired.
The bad news is, you've got one week to regain your jobs.
Starting with tonight's sit.
The leads are weak.
The leads are weak? Ruddy leads are weak?
YOU'RE WEAK.
I've been in this business 15 years...
Enough! Well done every-one, sit down.
Charlotte, you're Blake. That was very impressive.
Well I saw myself as *Shelley* really.
...but I accept.
Mr Beckwith, I *hear* Mrs B is in the family way.
Do you need a babysitter? Shauna here is a caring sort.
SAFE HANDS.
Lottie! It is MONTHS until Baby Beckwith! That was embarrassing!
He said he'd bear you in mind. ABC.
ALWAYS BE CLOSING.

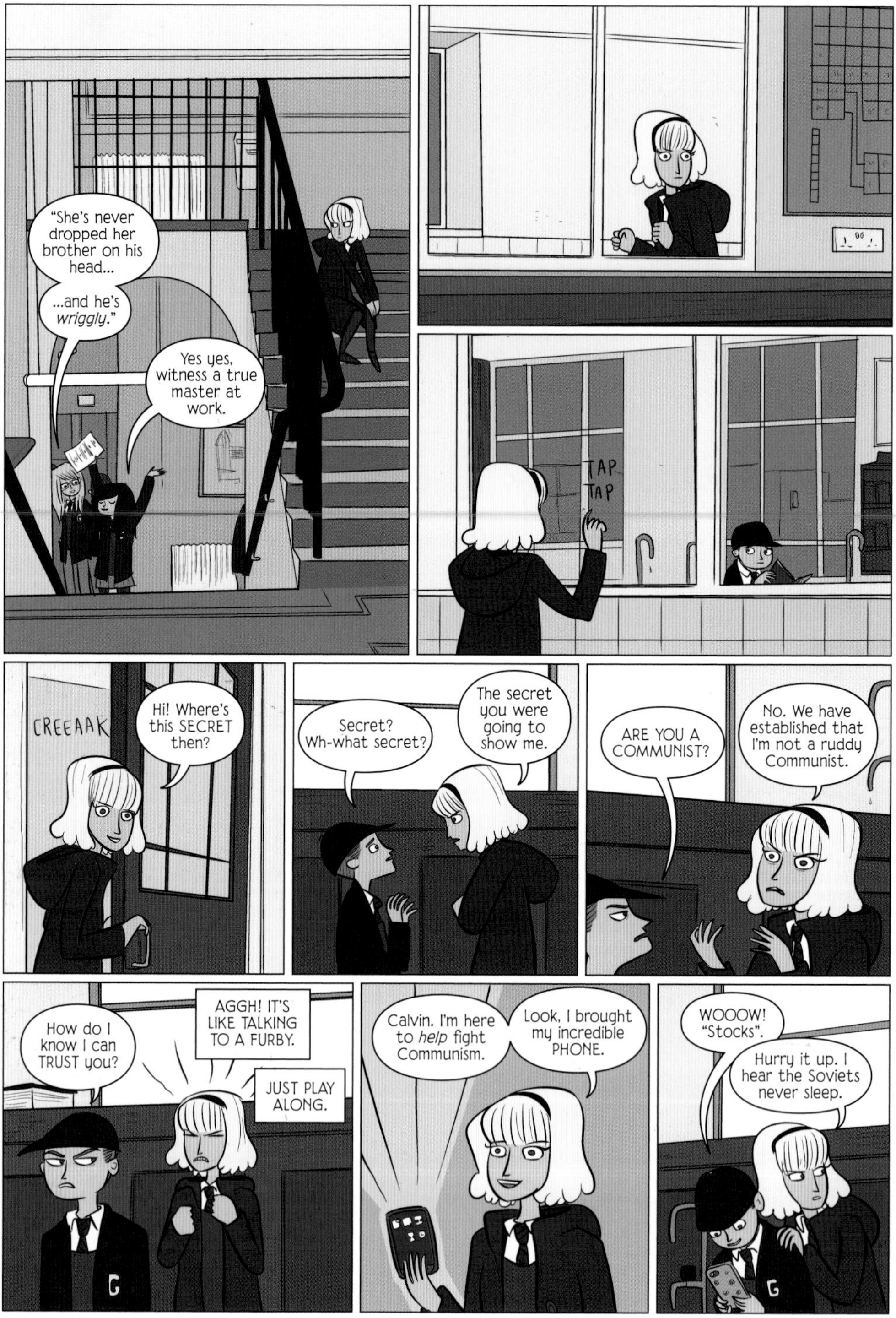
"She's never dropped her brother on his head...
...and he's *wriggly*."
Yes yes, witness a true master at work.
TAP TAP
CREEAAK
Hi! Where's this SECRET then?
Secret? Wh-what secret?
The secret you were going to show me.
ARE YOU A COMMUNIST?
No. We have established that I'm not a ruddy Communist.
How do I know I can TRUST you?
AGGH! IT'S LIKE TALKING TO A FURBY.
JUST PLAY ALONG.
Calvin. I'm here to *help* fight Communism.
Look, I brought my incredible PHONE.
WOOOW! "Stocks".
Hurry it up. I hear the Soviets never sleep.

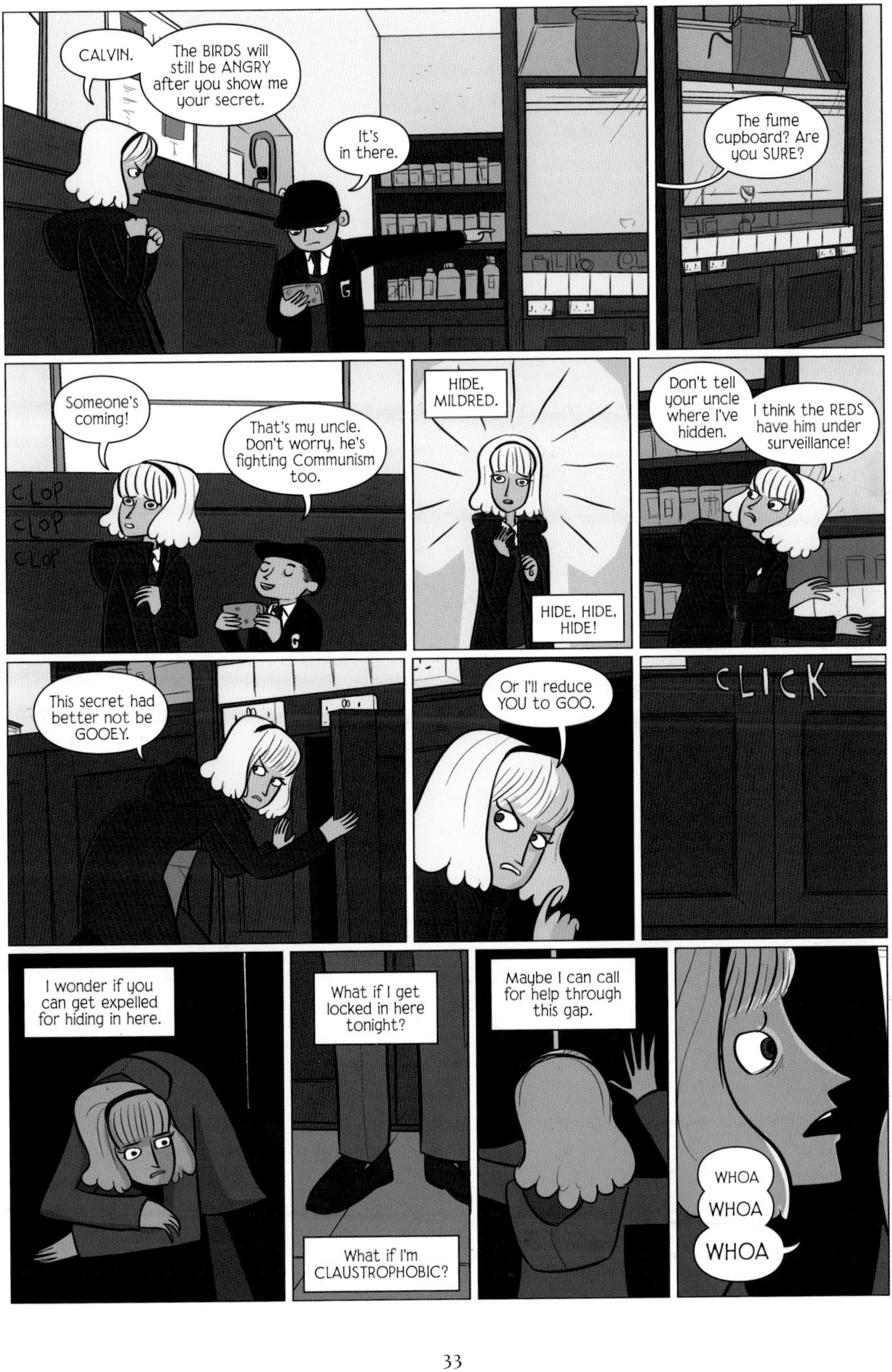
CALVIN.
The BIRDS will still be ANGRY after you show me your secret.
It's in there.
The fume cupboard? Are you SURE?
Someone's coming!
CLOP CLOP CLOP
That's my uncle. Don't worry, he's fighting Communism too.
HIDE, MILDRED.
HIDE, HIDE, HIDE!
Don't tell your uncle where I've hidden.
I think the REDS have him under surveillance!
This secret had better not be GOOEY.
Or I'll reduce YOU to GOO.
CLICK
I wonder if you can get expelled for hiding in here.
What if I get locked in here tonight?
What if I'm CLAUSTROPHOBIC?
Maybe I can call for help through this gap.
WHOA
WHOA
WHOA

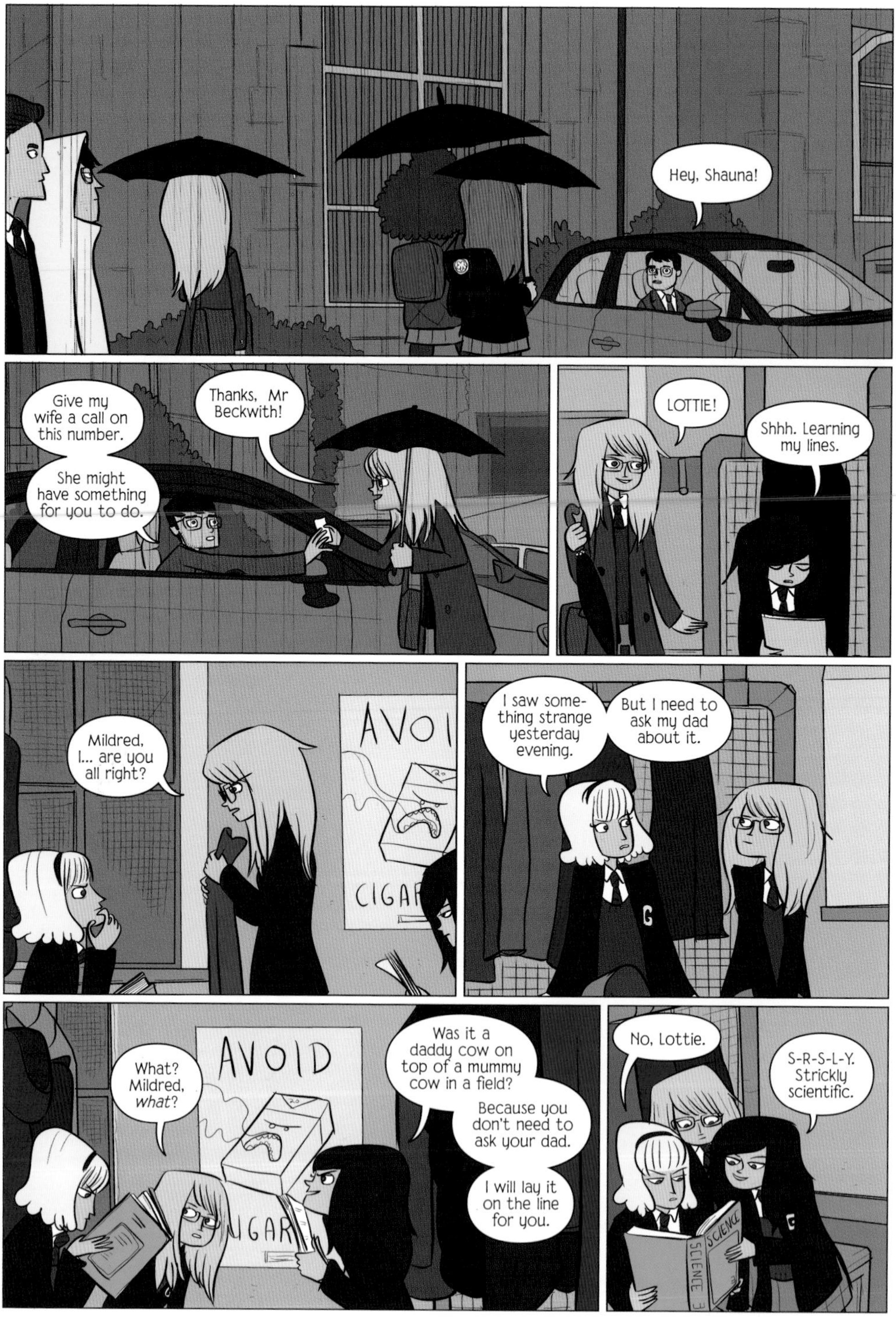
Hey, Shauna!
Give my wife a call on this number.
She might have something for you to do.
Thanks, Mr Beckwith!
LOTTIE!
Shhh. Learning my lines.
Mildred, I... are you all right?
AVOI
CIGAR
I saw something strange yesterday evening.
But I need to ask my dad about it.
What? Mildred, *what*?
AVOID
IGAR
Was it a daddy cow on top of a mummy cow in a field?
Because you don't need to ask your dad.
I will lay it on the line for you.
No, Lottie.
S-R-S-L-Y. Strickly scientific.
SCIENCE
SCIENCE 3

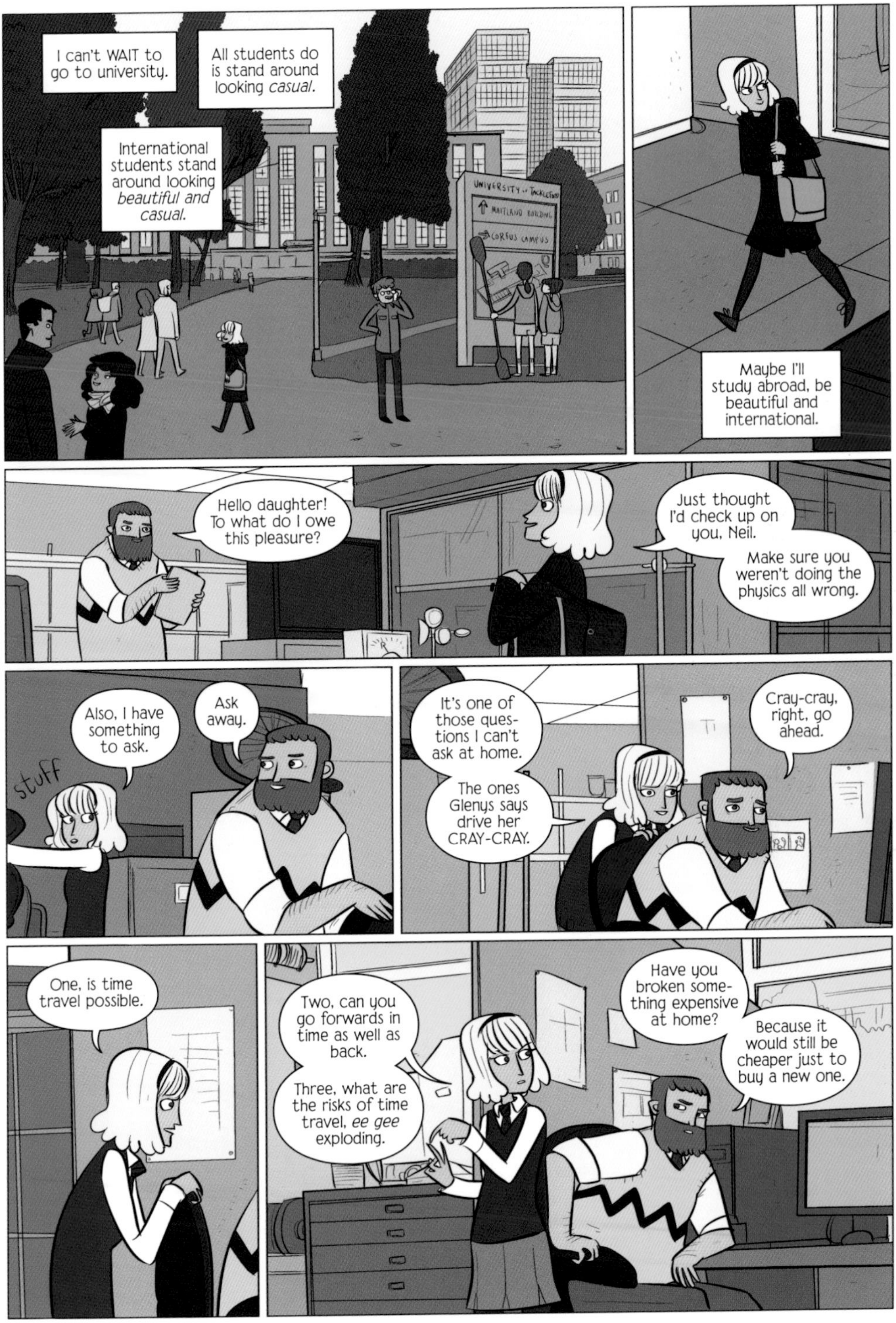
I can't WAIT to go to university.
All students do is stand around looking *casual.*
International students stand around looking *beautiful and casual.*
Maybe I'll study abroad, be beautiful and international.
Hello daughter! To what do I owe this pleasure?
Just thought I'd check up on you, Neil.
Make sure you weren't doing the physics all wrong.
Also, I have something to ask.
Ask away.
stuff
It's one of those ques- tions I can't ask at home.
The ones Glenys says drive her CRAY-CRAY.
Cray-cray, right, go ahead.
One, is time travel possible.
Two, can you go forwards in time as well as back.
Three, what are the risks of time travel, *ee gee* exploding.
Have you broken some- thing expensive at home?
Because it would still be cheaper just to buy a new one.

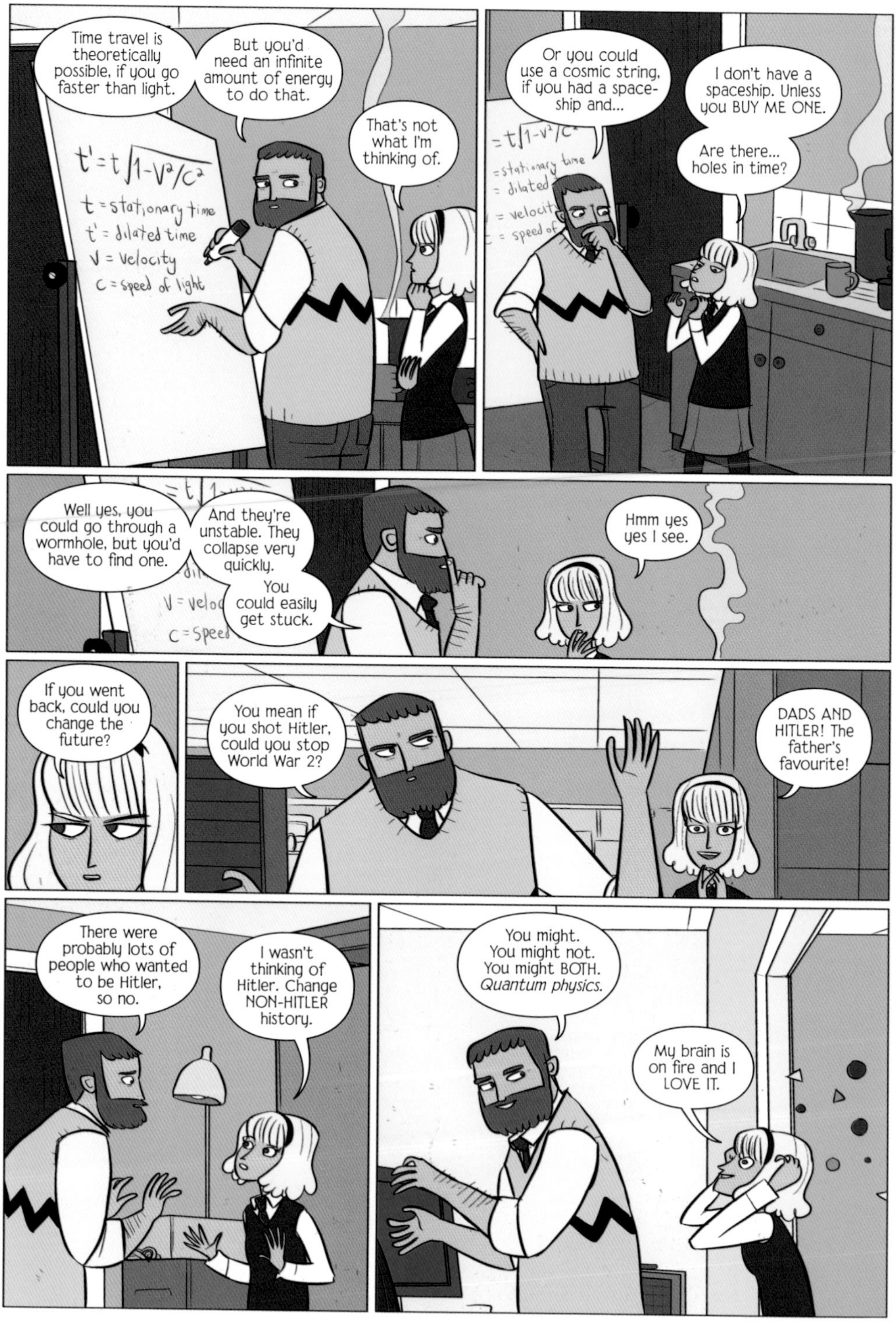
Time travel is theoretically possible, if you go faster than light.
But you'd need an infinite amount of energy to do that.
t' = t √(1-v²/c²)
t = stationary time
t' = dilated time
v = velocity
c = speed of light
That's not what I'm thinking of.
Or you could use a cosmic string, if you had a space-ship and...
I don't have a spaceship. Unless you BUY ME ONE.
Are there... holes in time?
Well yes, you could go through a wormhole, but you'd have to find one.
And they're unstable. They collapse very quickly.
You could easily get stuck.
Hmm yes yes I see.
If you went back, could you change the future?
You mean if you shot Hitler, could you stop World War 2?
DADS AND HITLER! The father's favourite!
There were probably lots of people who wanted to be Hitler, so no.
I wasn't thinking of Hitler. Change NON-HITLER history.
You might. You might not. You might BOTH. *Quantum physics.*
My brain is on fire and I LOVE IT.

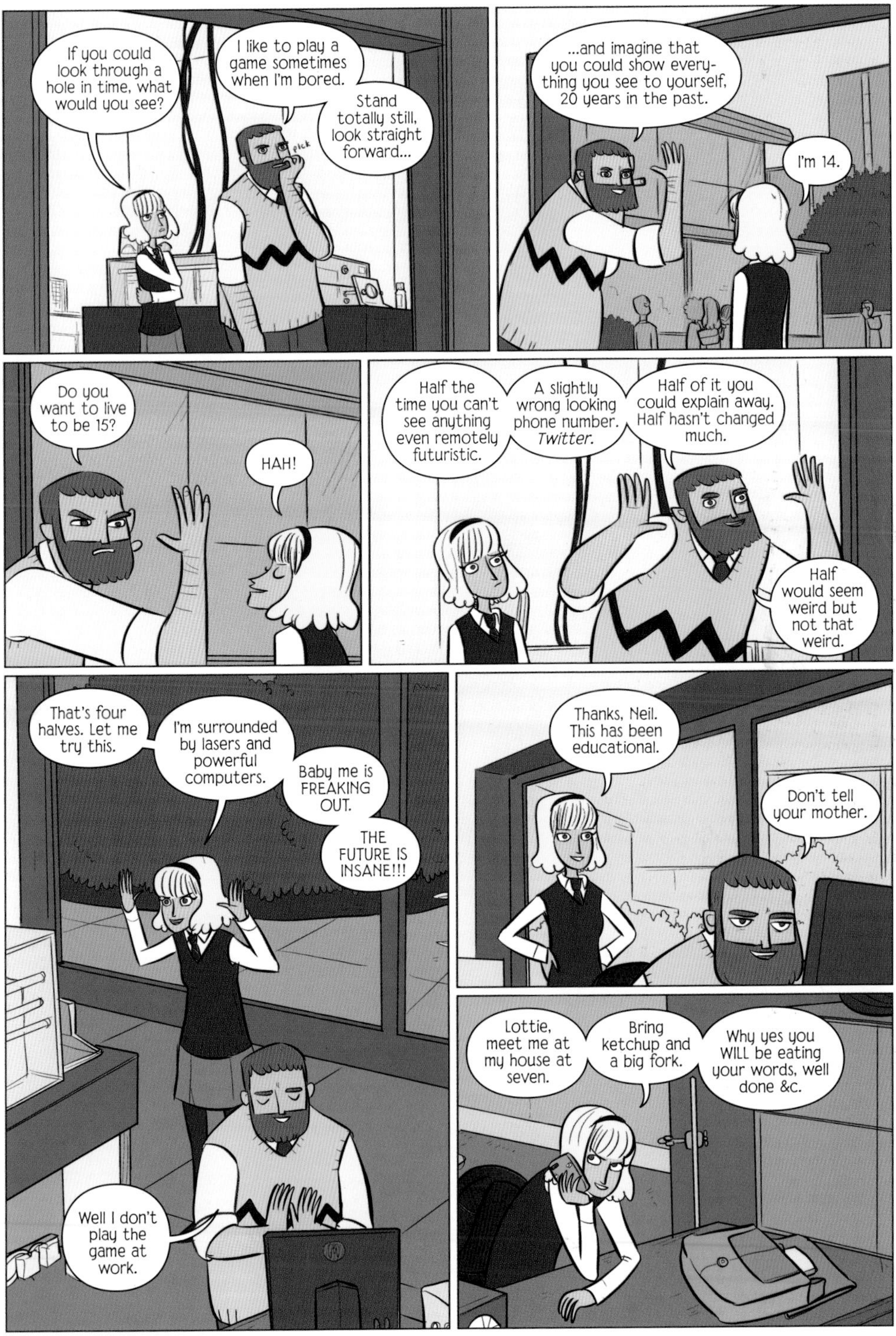
If you could look through a hole in time, what would you see?
I like to play a game sometimes when I'm bored.
Stand totally still, look straight forward...
pick
...and imagine that you could show every-thing you see to yourself, 20 years in the past.
I'm 14.
Do you want to live to be 15?
HAH!
Half the time you can't see anything even remotely futuristic.
A slightly wrong looking phone number. *Twitter.*
Half of it you could explain away. Half hasn't changed much.
Half would seem weird but not that weird.
That's four halves. Let me try this.
I'm surrounded by lasers and powerful computers.
Baby me is FREAKING OUT.
THE FUTURE IS INSANE!!!
Well I don't play the game at work.
Thanks, Neil. This has been educational.
Don't tell your mother.
Lottie, meet me at my house at seven.
Bring ketchup and a big fork.
Why yes you WILL be eating your words, well done &c.

2
(TWO)

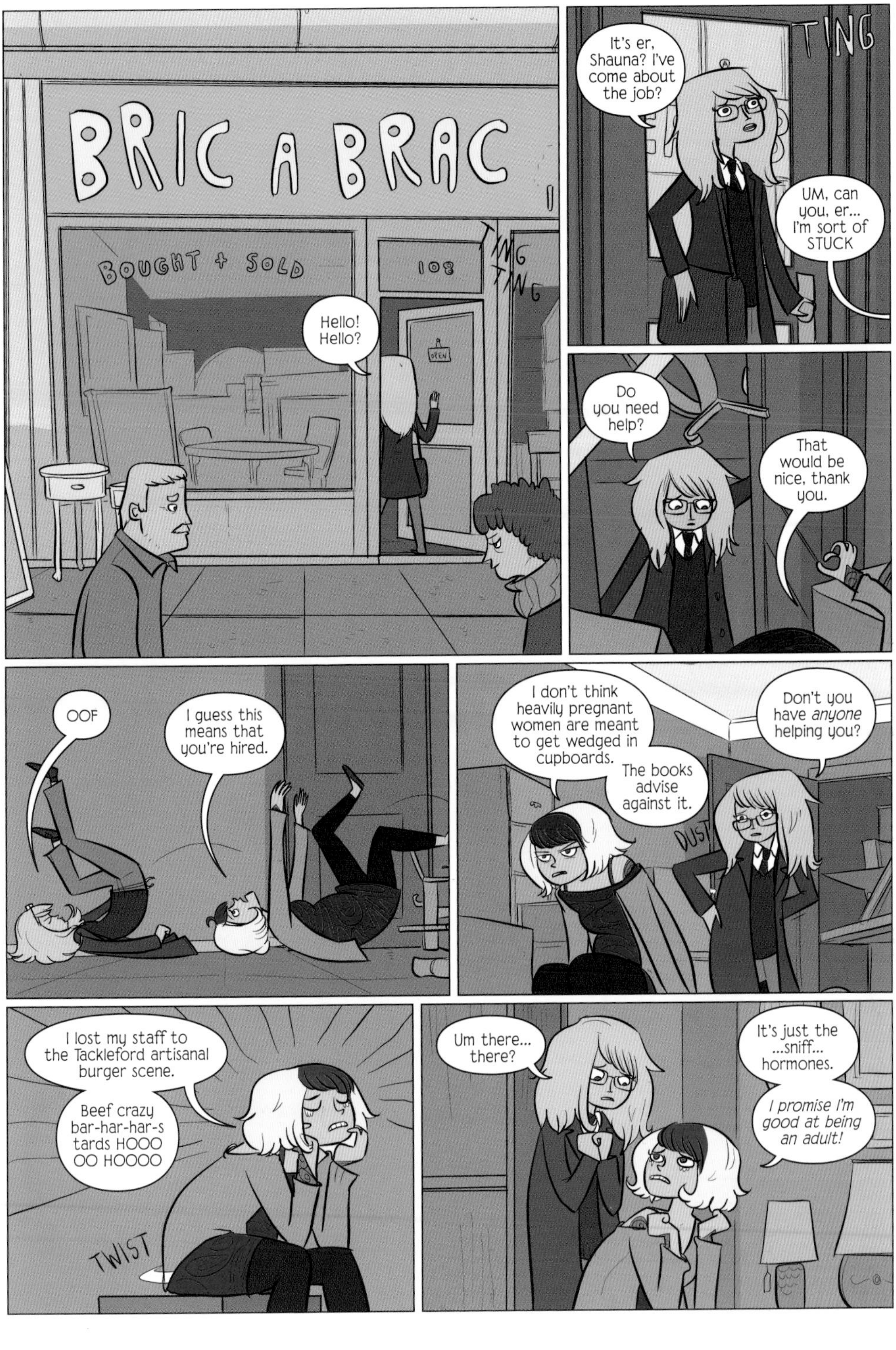
BRIC A BRAC
BOUGHT + SOLD
108
TING TING
Hello! Hello?
OPEN
It's er, Shauna? I've come about the job?
TING
UM, can you, er... I'm sort of STUCK
Do you need help?
That would be nice, thank you.
OOF
I guess this means that you're hired.
I don't think heavily pregnant women are meant to get wedged in cupboards.
The books advise against it.
Don't you have *anyone* helping you?
DUST
I lost my staff to the Tackleford artisanal burger scene.
Beef crazy bar-har-har-s tards HOOO OO HOOOO
TWIST
Um there... there?
It's just the ...sniff... hormones.
I promise I'm good at being an adult!

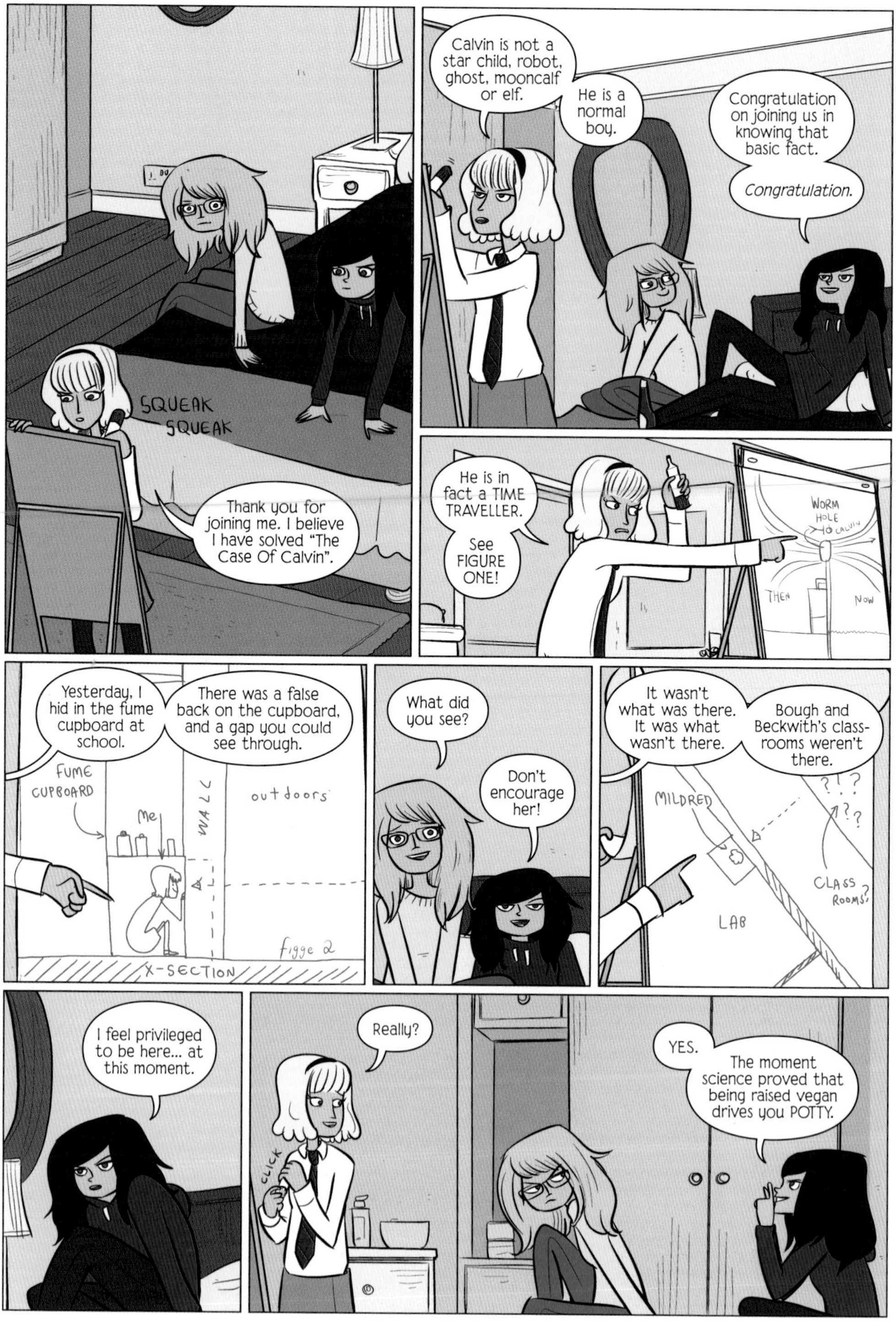
SQUEAK
SQUEAK
Thank you for joining me. I believe I have solved "The Case Of Calvin".
Calvin is not a star child, robot, ghost, mooncalf or elf.
He is a normal boy.
Congratulation on joining us in knowing that basic fact.
Congratulation.
He is in fact a TIME TRAVELLER.
See FIGURE ONE!
WORM HOLE
TO CALVIN
THEN
NOW
Yesterday, I hid in the fume cupboard at school.
There was a false back on the cupboard, and a gap you could see through.
FUME CUPBOARD
ME
WALL
outdoors
X-SECTION
What did you see?
Don't encourage her!
It wasn't what was there. It was what wasn't there.
Bough and Beckwith's class-rooms weren't there.
MILDRED
LAB
CLASS ROOMS?
I feel privileged to be here... at this moment.
Really?
CLICK
YES.
The moment science proved that being raised vegan drives you POTTY.

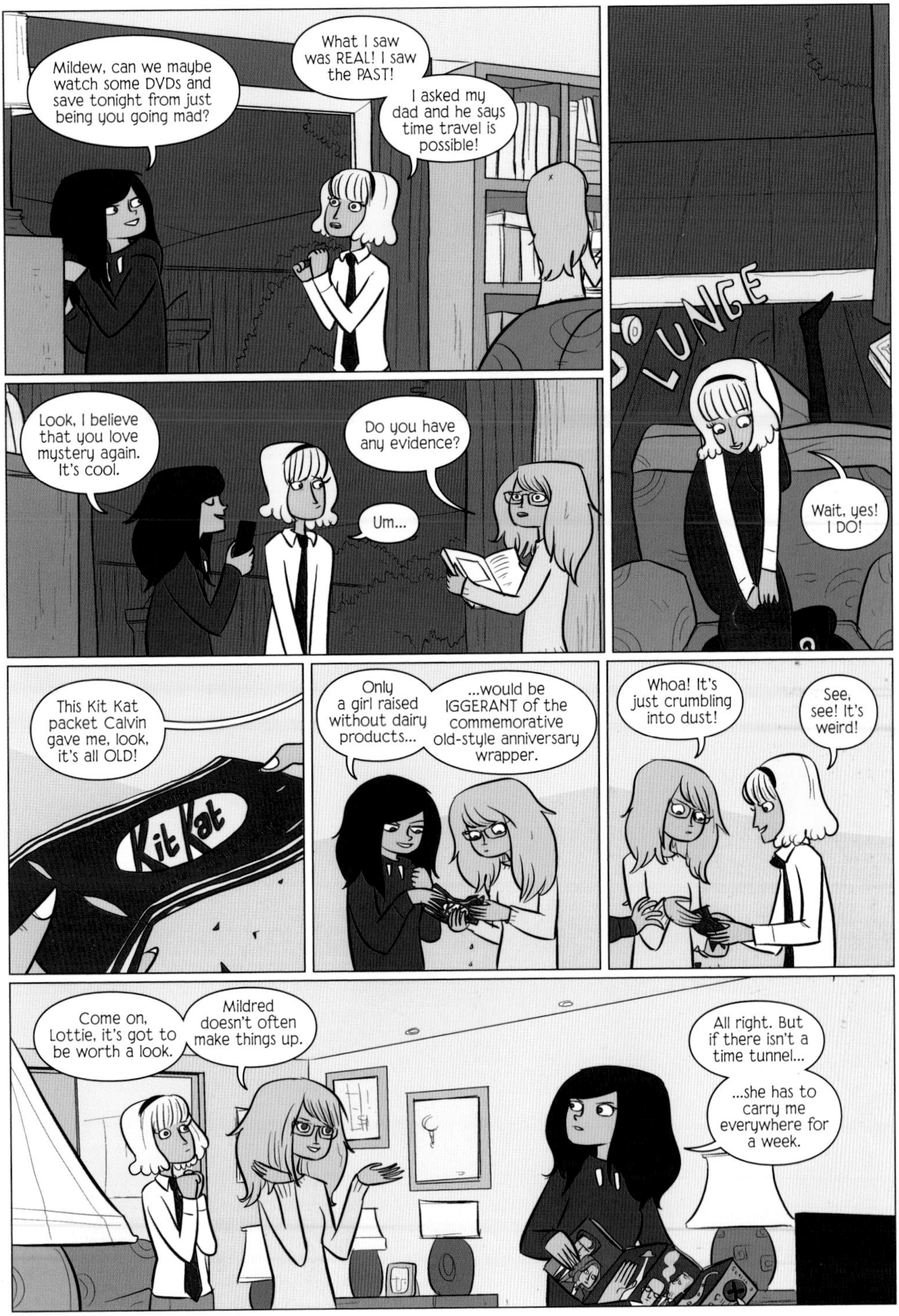
Mildew, can we maybe watch some DVDs and save tonight from just being you going mad?
What I saw was REAL! I saw the PAST!
I asked my dad and he says time travel is possible!
Look, I believe that you love mystery again. It's cool.
Do you have any evidence?
Um...
Wait, yes! I DO!
This Kit Kat packet Calvin gave me, look, it's all OLD!
Kit Kat
Only a girl raised without dairy products...
...would be IGGERANT of the commemorative old-style anniversary wrapper.
Whoa! It's just crumbling into dust!
See, see! It's weird!
Come on, Lottie, it's got to be worth a look.
Mildred doesn't often make things up.
All right. But if there isn't a time tunnel...
...she has to carry me everywhere for a week.

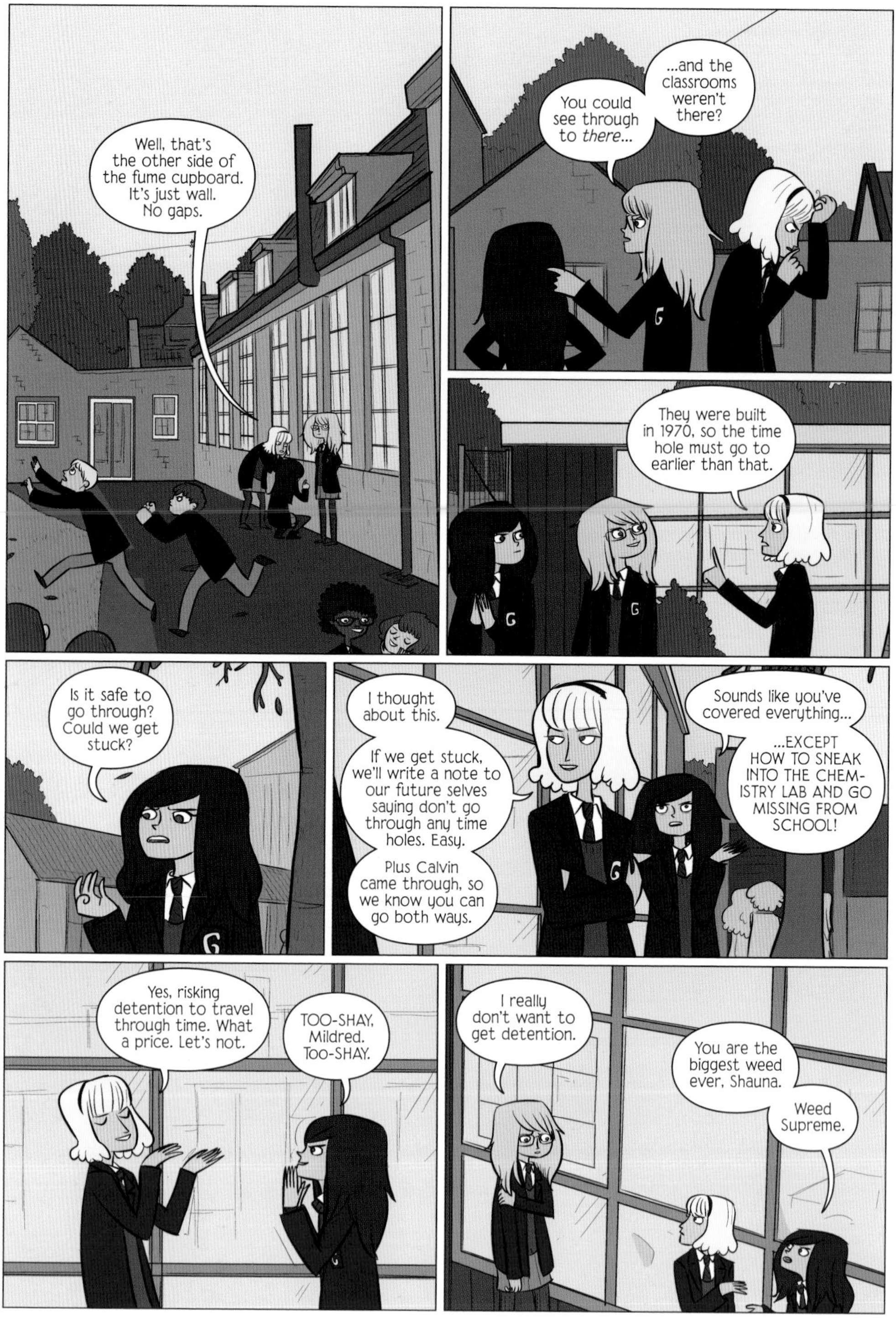
Well, that's the other side of the fume cupboard. It's just wall. No gaps.
You could see through to *there*...
...and the classrooms weren't there?
They were built in 1970, so the time hole must go to earlier than that.
Is it safe to go through? Could we get stuck?
I thought about this.
If we get stuck, we'll write a note to our future selves saying don't go through any time holes. Easy.
Plus Calvin came through, so we know you can go both ways.
Sounds like you've covered everything...
...EXCEPT HOW TO SNEAK INTO THE CHEMISTRY LAB AND GO MISSING FROM SCHOOL!
Yes, risking detention to travel through time. What a price. Let's not.
TOO-SHAY, Mildred. Too-SHAY.
I really don't want to get detention.
You are the biggest weed ever, Shauna.
Weed Supreme.

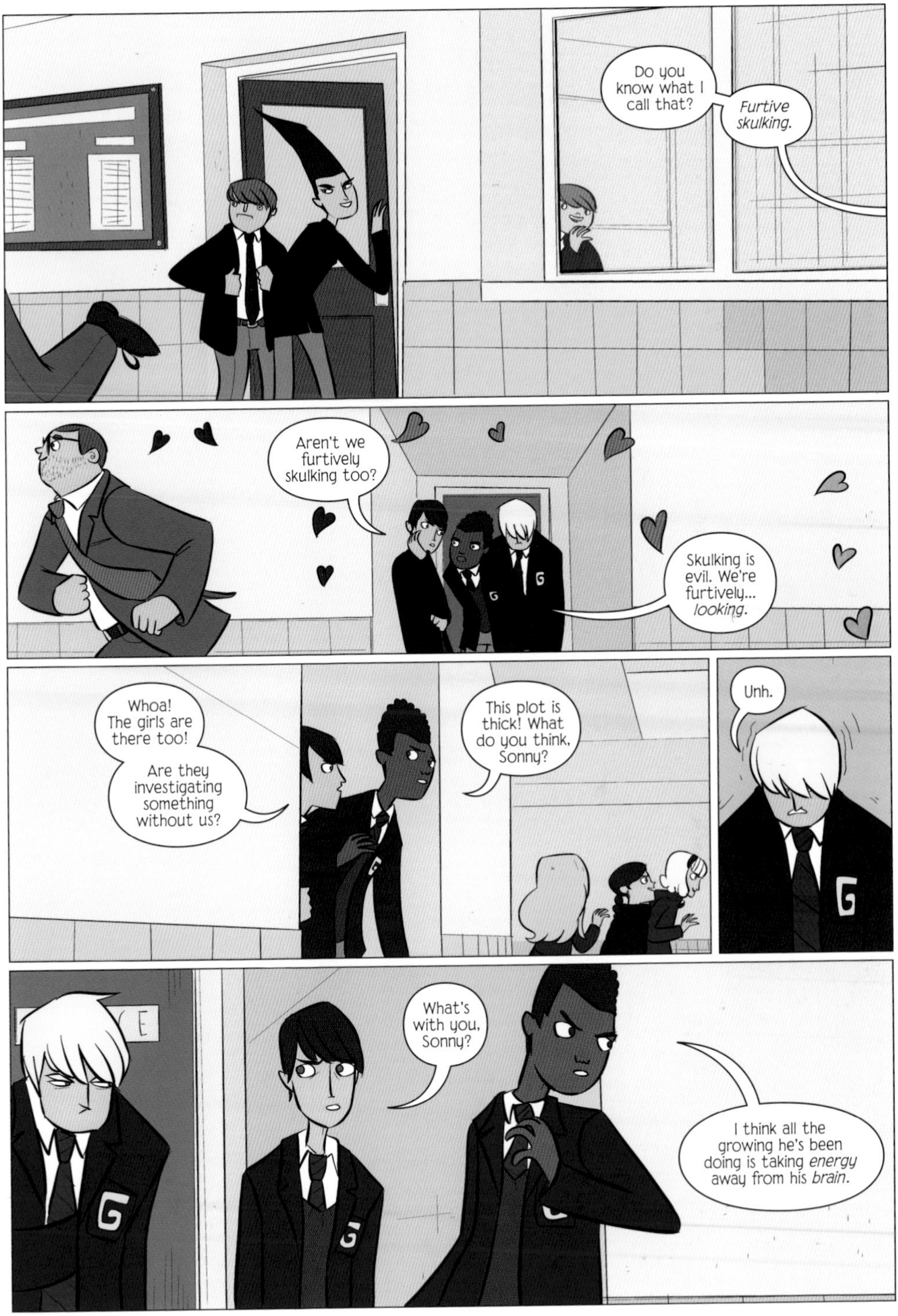
Do you know what I call that?
Furtive skulking.
Aren't we furtively skulking too?
Skulking is evil. We're furtively... looking.
Whoa! The girls are there too!
Are they investigating something without us?
This plot is thick! What do you think, Sonny?
Unh.
What's with you, Sonny?
I think all the growing he's been doing is taking energy away from his brain.

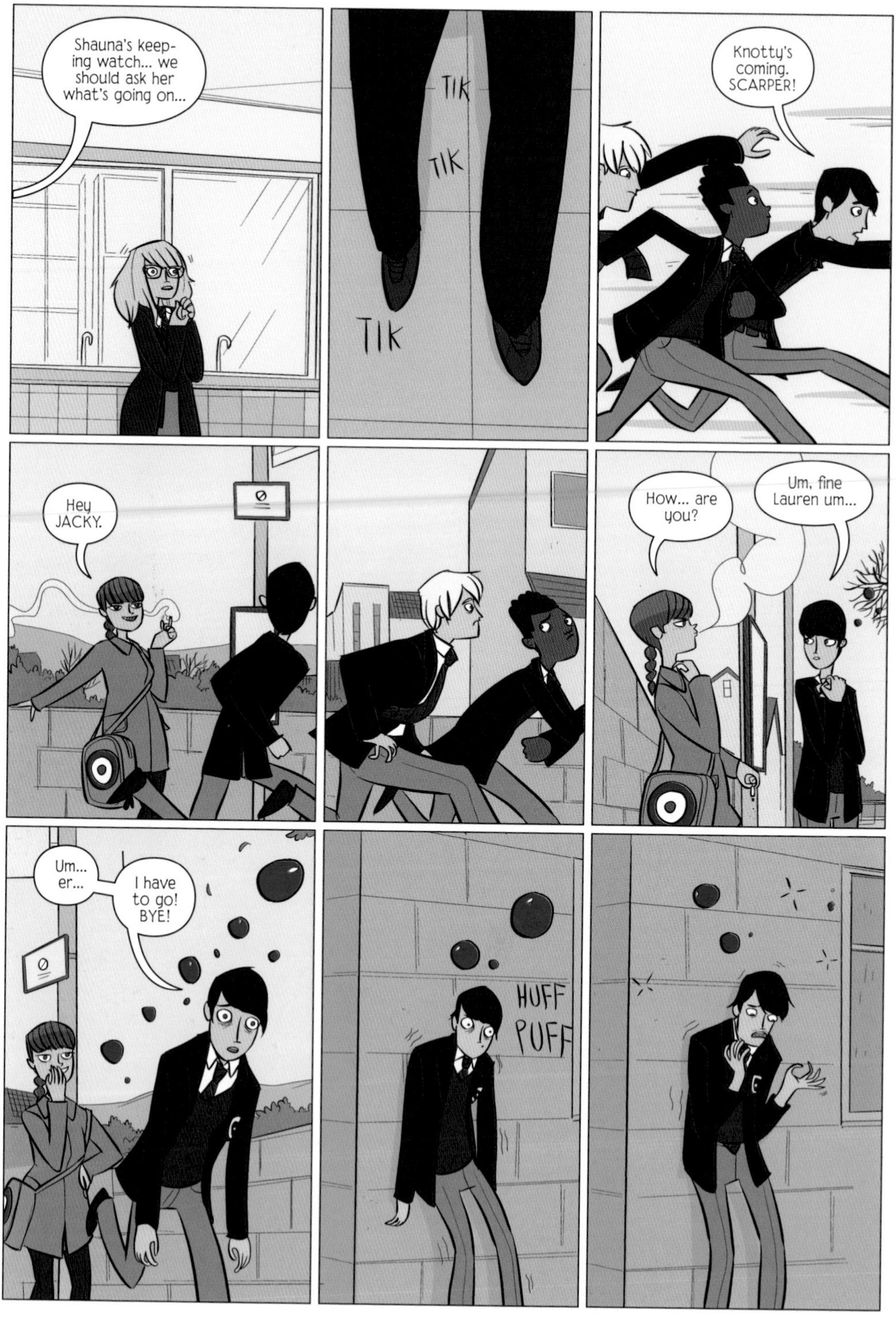
Shauna's keep-ing watch... we should ask her what's going on...
TIK
TIK
TIK
Knotty's coming. SCARPER!
Hey JACKY.
How... are you?
Um, fine Lauren um...
Um... er...
I have to go! BYE!
HUFF
PUFF

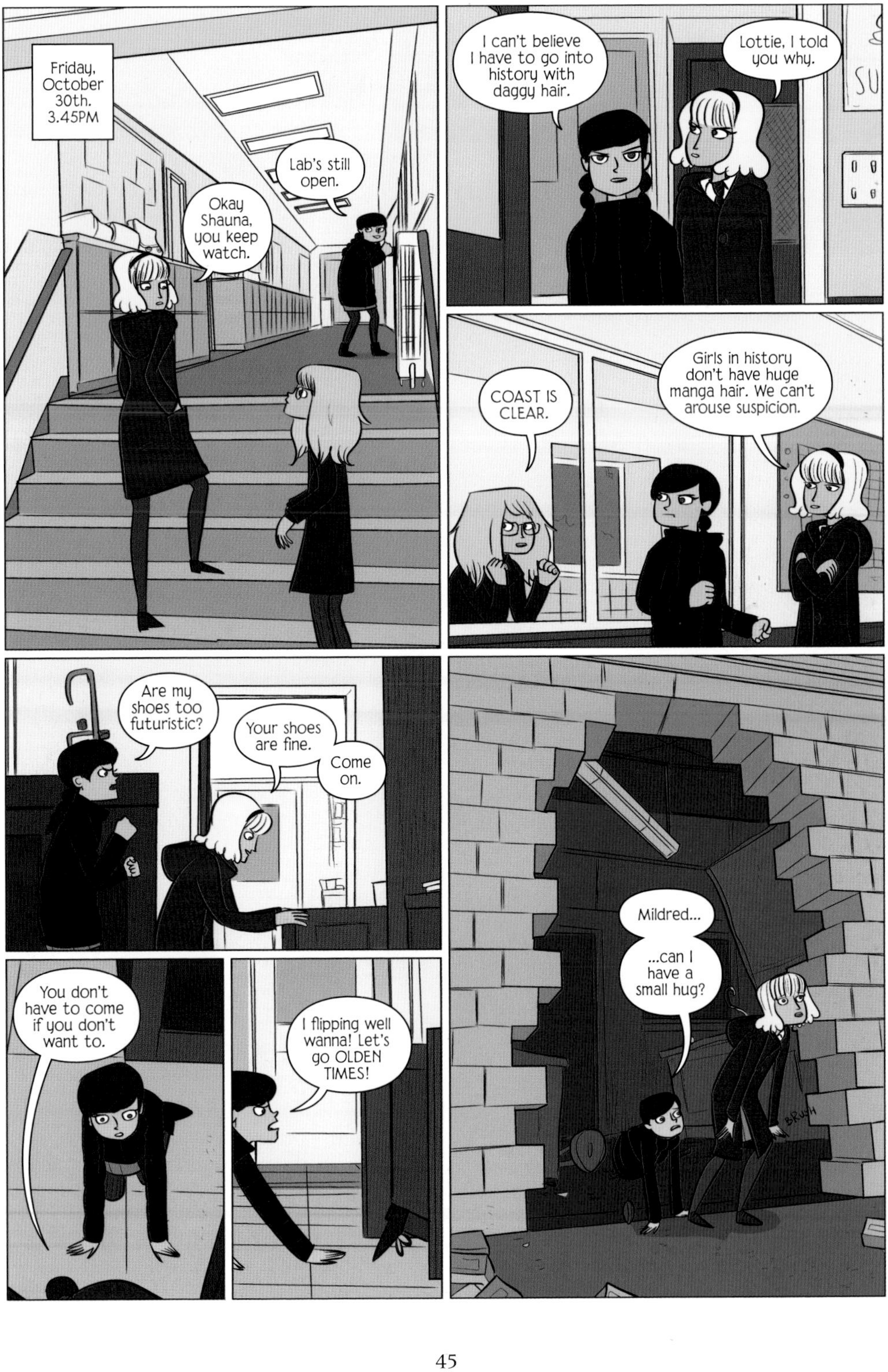
Friday, October 30th. 3.45PM
Lab's still open.
Okay Shauna, you keep watch.
I can't believe I have to go into history with daggy hair.
Lottie, I told you why.
COAST IS CLEAR.
Girls in history don't have huge manga hair. We can't arouse suspicion.
Are my shoes too futuristic?
Your shoes are fine.
Come on.
You don't have to come if you don't want to.
I flipping well wanna! Let's go OLDEN TIMES!
Mildred...
...can I have a small hug?
BRUSH

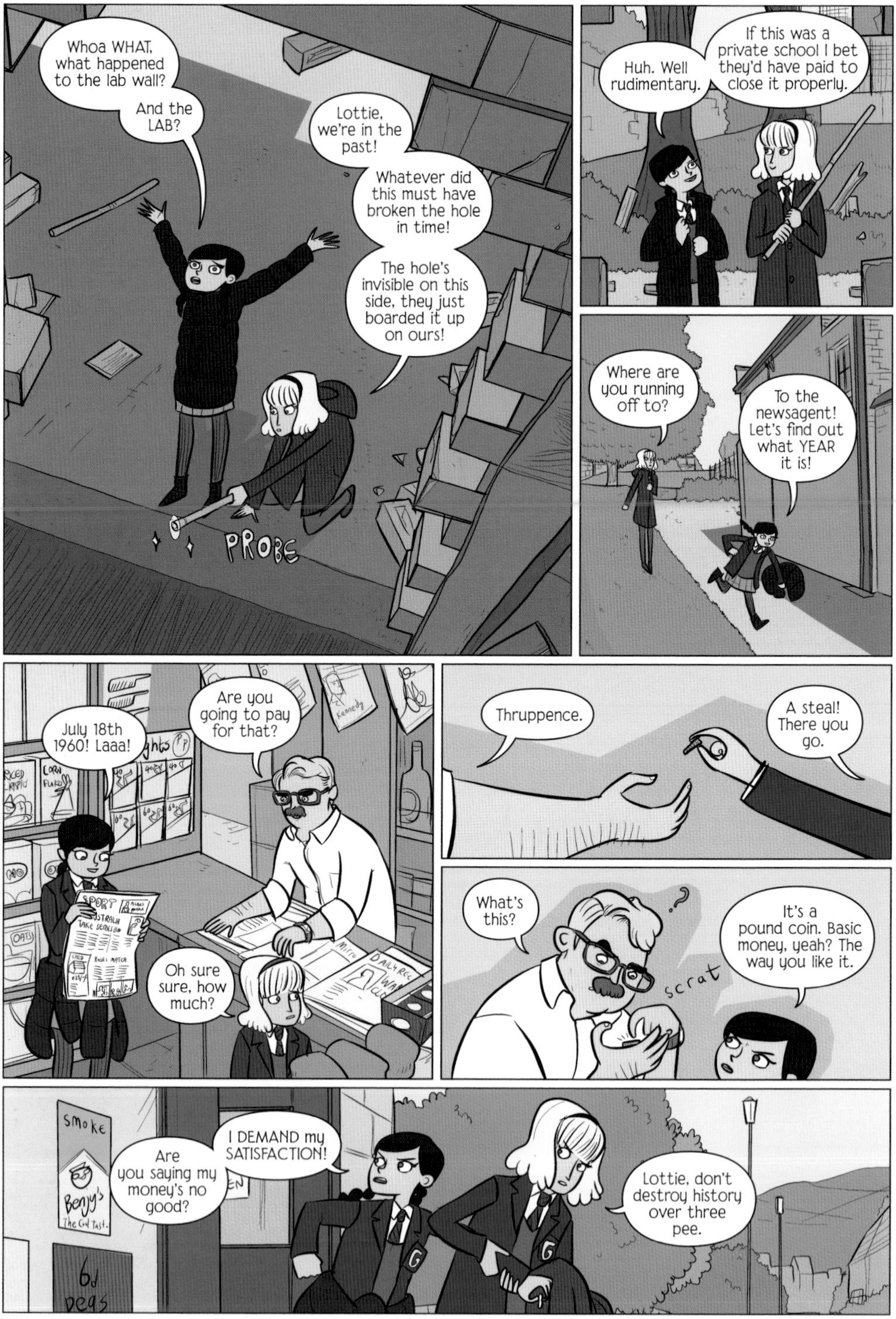
Whoa WHAT, what happened to the lab wall?
And the LAB?
Lottie, we're in the past!
Whatever did this must have broken the hole in time!
The hole's invisible on this side, they just boarded it up on ours!
PROBE
Huh. Well rudimentary.
If this was a private school I bet they'd have paid to close it properly.
Where are you running off to?
To the newsagent! Let's find out what YEAR it is!
July 18th 1960! Laaa!
Are you going to pay for that?
Oh sure sure, how much?
Thruppence.
A steal! There you go.
What's this?
It's a pound coin. Basic money, yeah? The way you like it.
scrat
Are you saying my money's no good?
I DEMAND my SATISFACTION!
Lottie, don't destroy history over three pee.

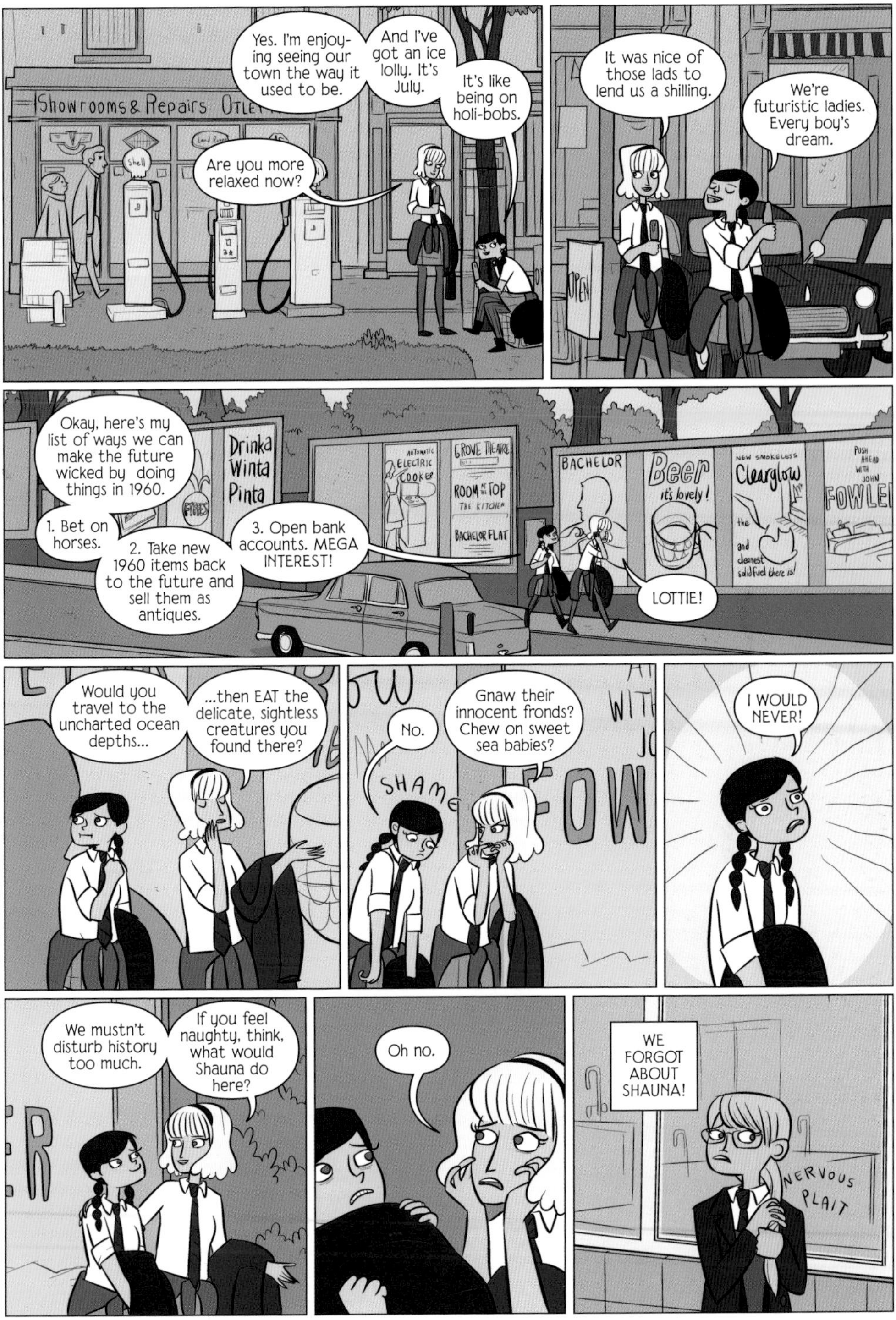
Showrooms & Repairs
Yes. I'm enjoying seeing our town the way it used to be.
And I've got an ice lolly. It's July.
It's like being on holi-bobs.
Are you more relaxed now?
It was nice of those lads to lend us a shilling.
We're futuristic ladies. Every boy's dream.
OPEN
Okay, here's my list of ways we can make the future wicked by doing things in 1960.
1. Bet on horses.
2. Take new 1960 items back to the future and sell them as antiques.
3. Open bank accounts. MEGA INTEREST!
Drinka Winta Pinta
AUTOMATIC ELECTRIC COOKER
GROVE THEATRE
ROOM AT THE TOP
BACHELOR FLAT
BACHELOR
Beer it's lovely!
NEW SMOKELESS Clearglow the cleanest solid fuel there is!
PUSH AHEAD WITH JOHN FOWLER
LOTTIE!
Would you travel to the uncharted ocean depths...
...then EAT the delicate, sightless creatures you found there?
No.
SHAME
Gnaw their innocent fronds? Chew on sweet sea babies?
I WOULD NEVER!
We mustn't disturb history too much.
If you feel naughty, think, what would Shauna do here?
Oh no.
WE FORGOT ABOUT SHAUNA!
NERVOUS PLAIT

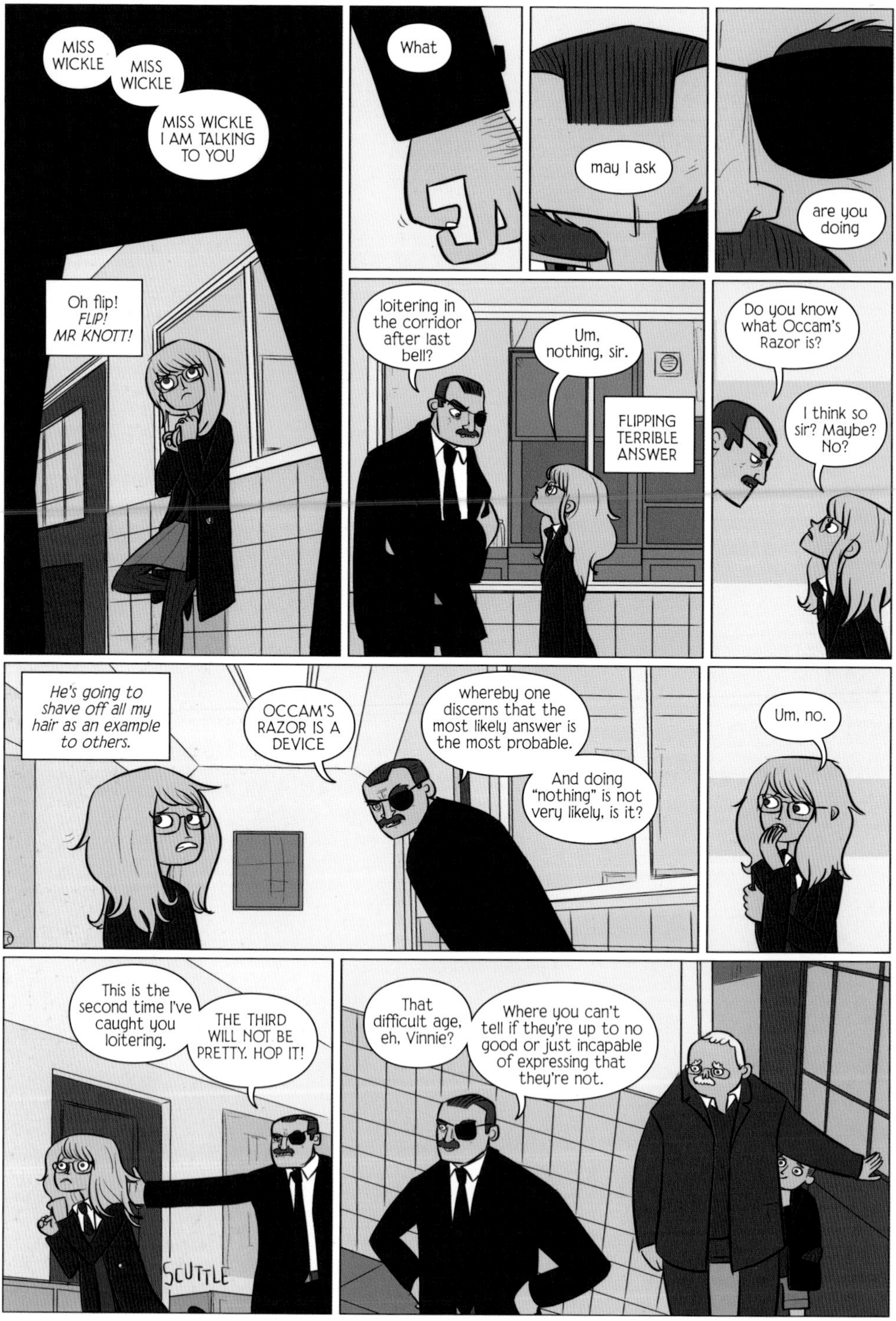
MISS WICKLE
MISS WICKLE
MISS WICKLE I AM TALKING TO YOU
Oh flip! FLIP! MR KNOTT!
What
may I ask
are you doing
loitering in the corridor after last bell?
Um, nothing, sir.
FLIPPING TERRIBLE ANSWER
Do you know what Occam's Razor is?
I think so sir? Maybe? No?
He's going to shave off all my hair as an example to others.
OCCAM'S RAZOR IS A DEVICE
whereby one discerns that the most likely answer is the most probable.
And doing "nothing" is not very likely, is it?
Um, no.
This is the second time I've caught you loitering.
THE THIRD WILL NOT BE PRETTY. HOP IT!
SCUTTLE
That difficult age, eh, Vinnie?
Where you can't tell if they're up to no good or just incapable of expressing that they're not.

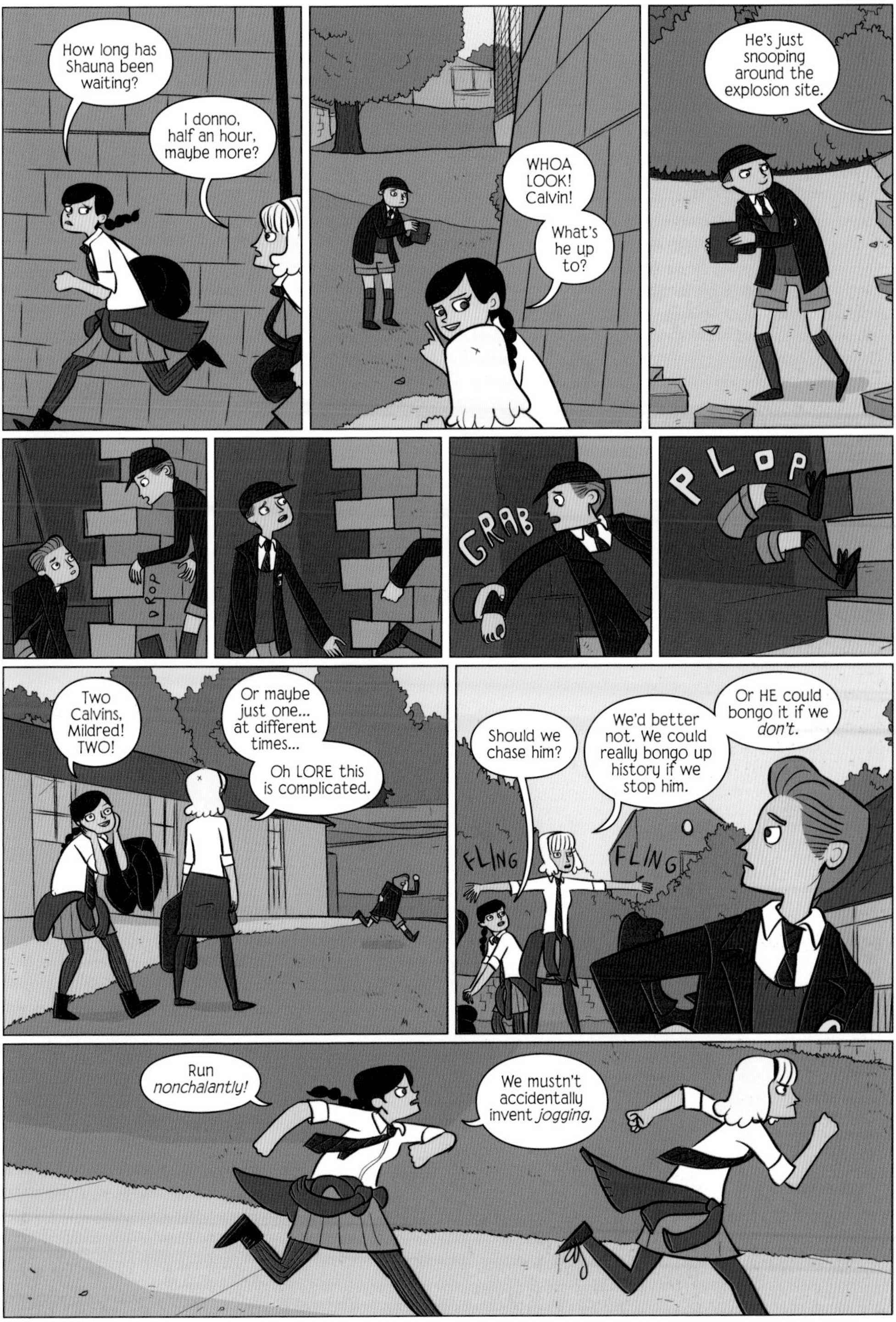
How long has Shauna been waiting?
I donno, half an hour, maybe more?
WHOA LOOK! Calvin!
What's he up to?
He's just snooping around the explosion site.
DROP
GRAB
PLOP
Two Calvins, Mildred! TWO!
Or maybe just one... at different times...
Oh LORE this is complicated.
Should we chase him?
We'd better not. We could really bongo up history if we stop him.
Or HE could bongo it if we *don't*.
FLING
FLING
Run *nonchalantly!*
We mustn't accidentally invent *jogging*.

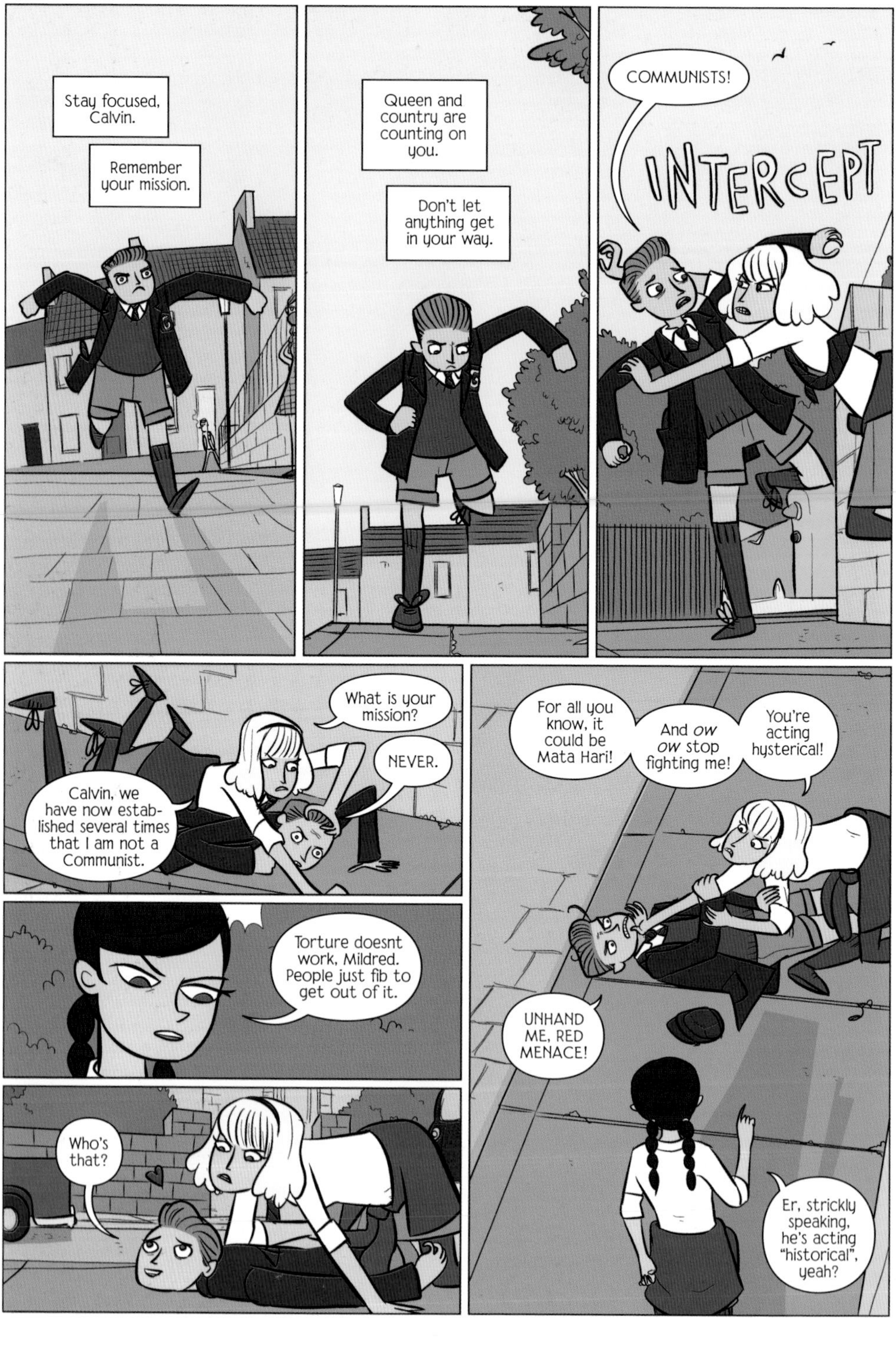
Stay focused, Calvin.
Remember your mission.
Queen and country are counting on you.
Don't let anything get in your way.
COMMUNISTS!
INTERCEPT
What is your mission?
NEVER.
Calvin, we have now established several times that I am not a Communist.
Torture doesnt work, Mildred. People just fib to get out of it.
Who's that?
For all you know, it could be Mata Hari!
And *ow ow* stop fighting me!
You're acting hysterical!
UNHAND ME, RED MENACE!
Er, strickly speaking, he's acting "historical", yeah?

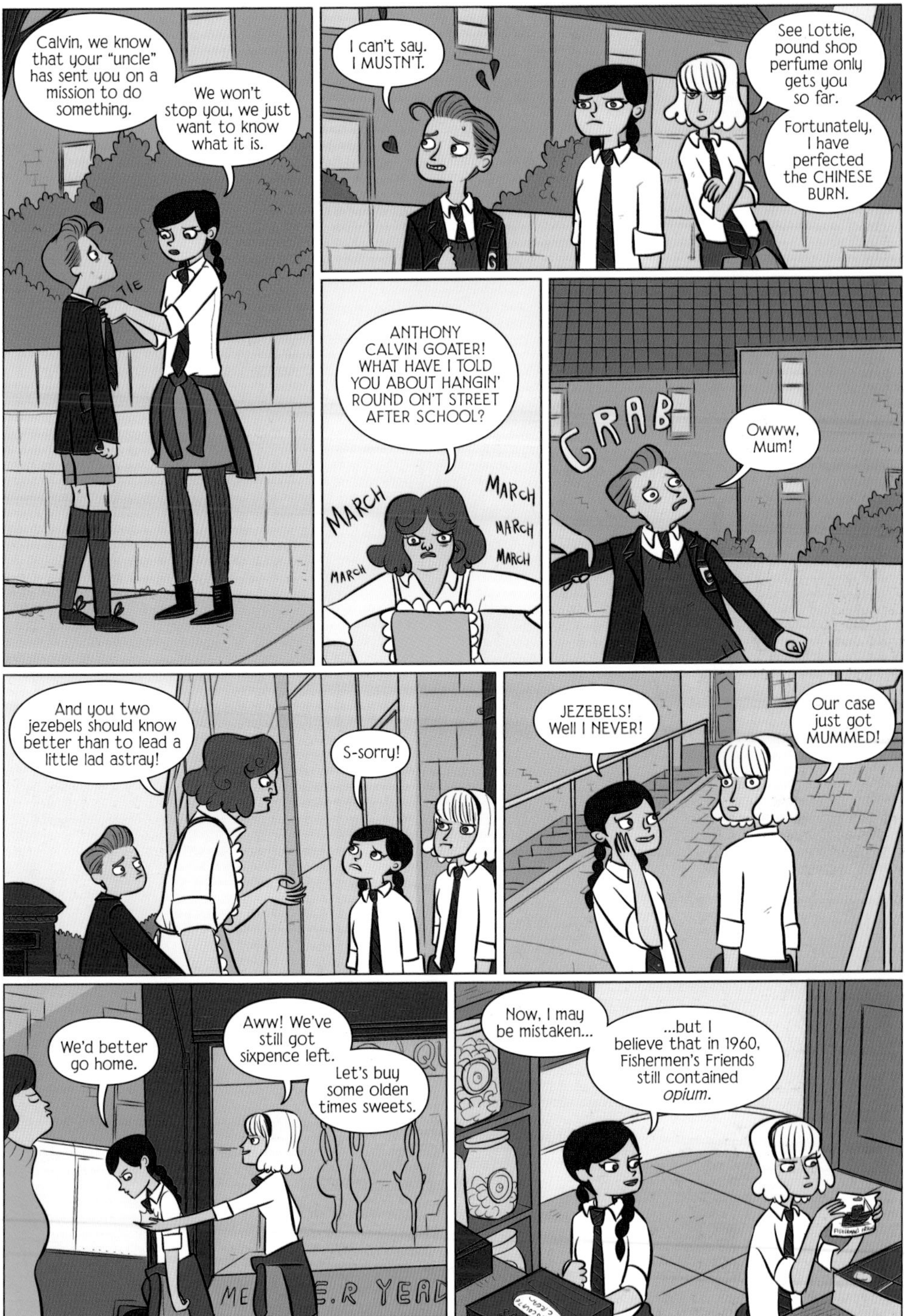
Calvin, we know that your "uncle" has sent you on a mission to do something.
We won't stop you, we just want to know what it is.
TIE
I can't say. I MUSTN'T.
See Lottie, pound shop perfume only gets you so far.
Fortunately, I have perfected the CHINESE BURN.
ANTHONY CALVIN GOATER! WHAT HAVE I TOLD YOU ABOUT HANGIN' ROUND ON'T STREET AFTER SCHOOL?
MARCH
MARCH
MARCH
MARCH
MARCH
GRAB
Owww, Mum!
And you two jezebels should know better than to lead a little lad astray!
S-sorry!
JEZEBELS! Well I NEVER!
Our case just got MUMMED!
We'd better go home.
Aww! We've still got sixpence left.
Let's buy some olden times sweets.
Now, I may be mistaken...
...but I believe that in 1960, Fishermen's Friends still contained *opium*.

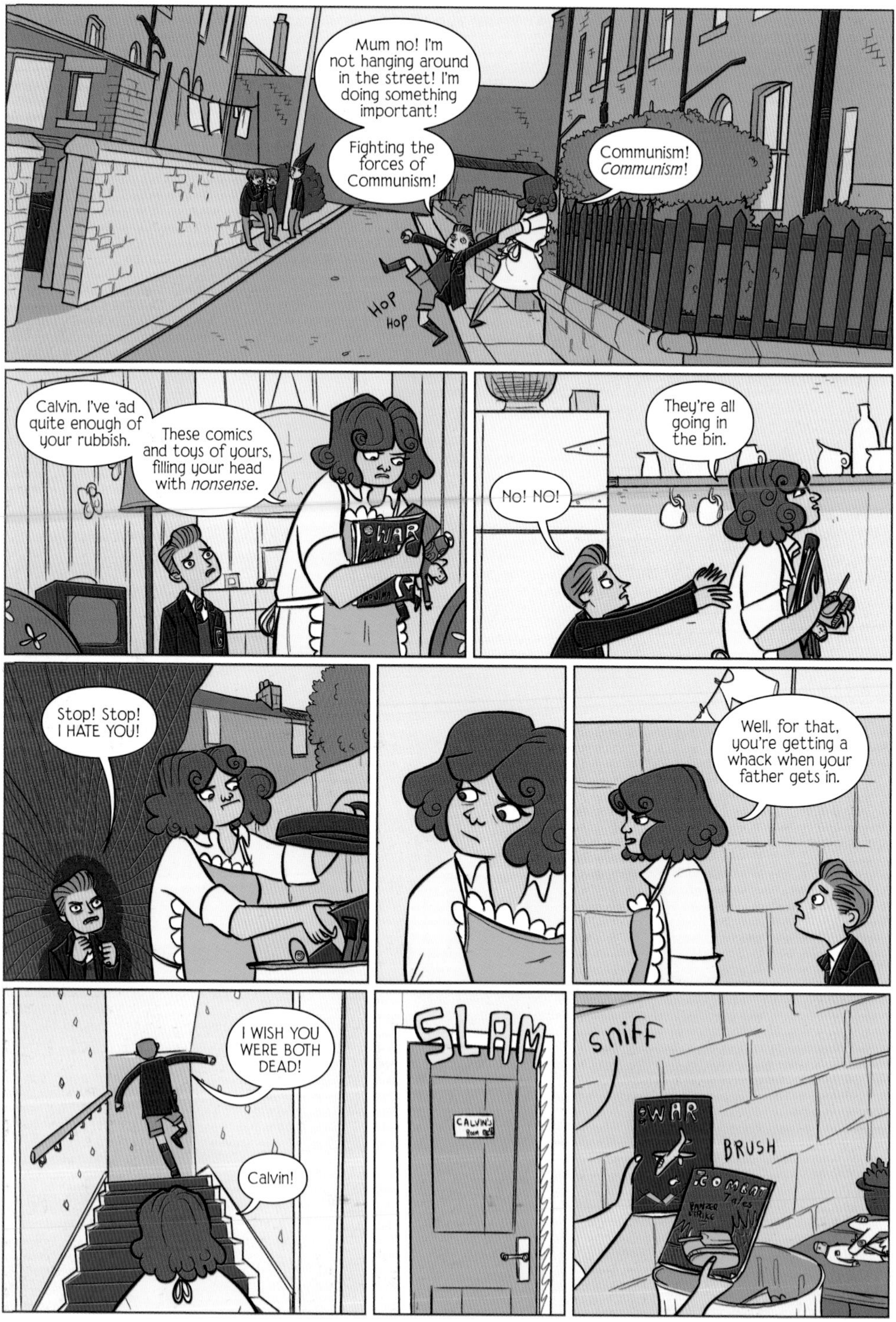
Mum no! I'm not hanging around in the street! I'm doing something important!
Fighting the forces of Communism!
Communism! *Communism*!
HOP HOP
Calvin. I've 'ad quite enough of your rubbish.
These comics and toys of yours, filling your head with *nonsense*.
WAR
They're all going in the bin.
No! NO!
Stop! Stop! I HATE YOU!
Well, for that, you're getting a whack when your father gets in.
I WISH YOU WERE BOTH DEAD!
Calvin!
SLAM
sniff
WAR
BRUSH
COMBAT Tales

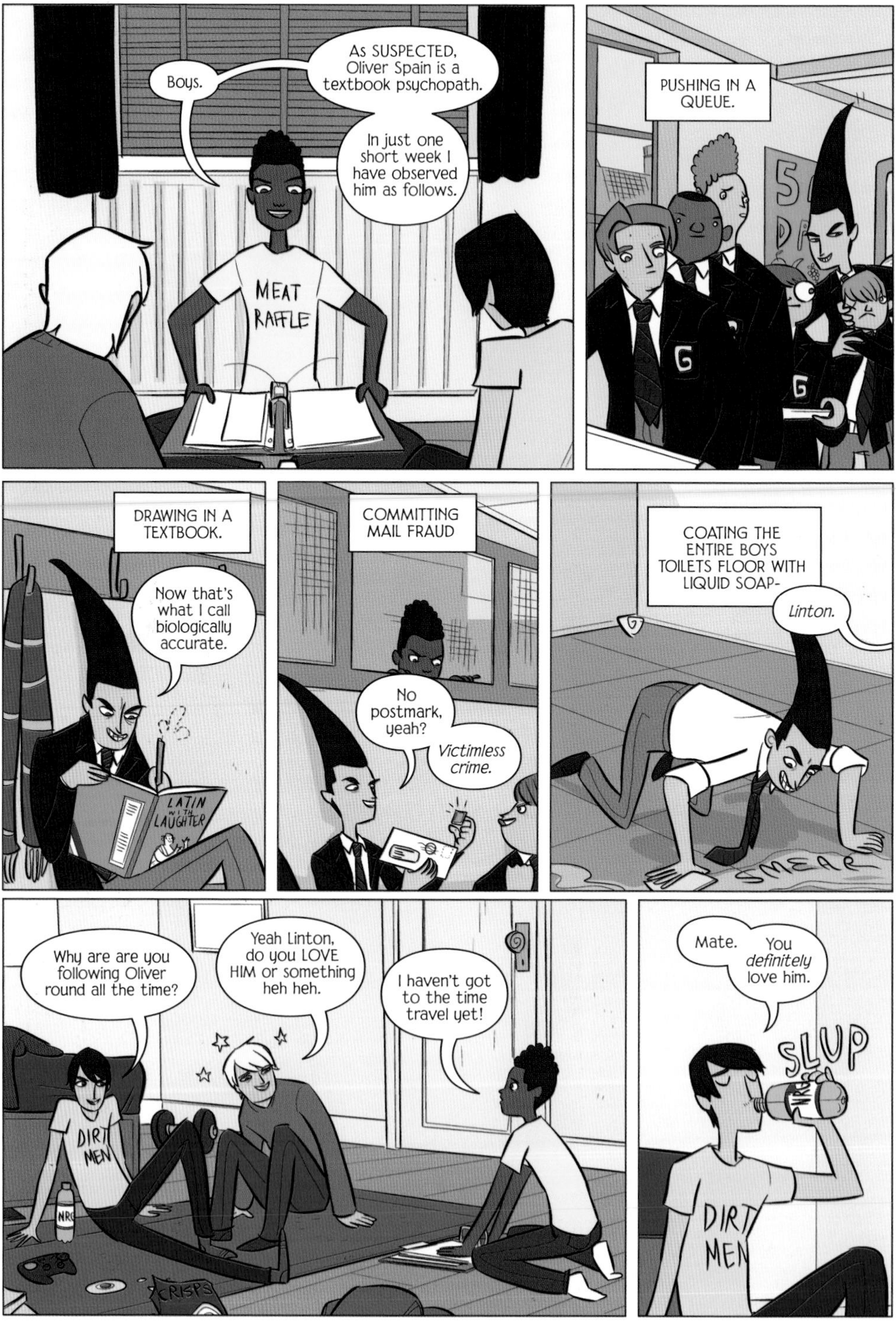
Boys.
As SUSPECTED, Oliver Spain is a textbook psychopath.
In just one short week I have observed him as follows.
MEAT RAFFLE
PUSHING IN A QUEUE.
DRAWING IN A TEXTBOOK.
Now that's what I call biologically accurate.
LATIN WITH LAUGHTER
COMMITTING MAIL FRAUD
No postmark, yeah?
Victimless crime.
COATING THE ENTIRE BOYS TOILETS FLOOR WITH LIQUID SOAP-
Linton.
SMEAR
Why are are you following Oliver round all the time?
Yeah Linton, do you LOVE HIM or something heh heh.
I haven't got to the time travel yet!
DIRT MEN
CRISPS
Mate.
You definitely love him.
SLUP
DIRT MEN

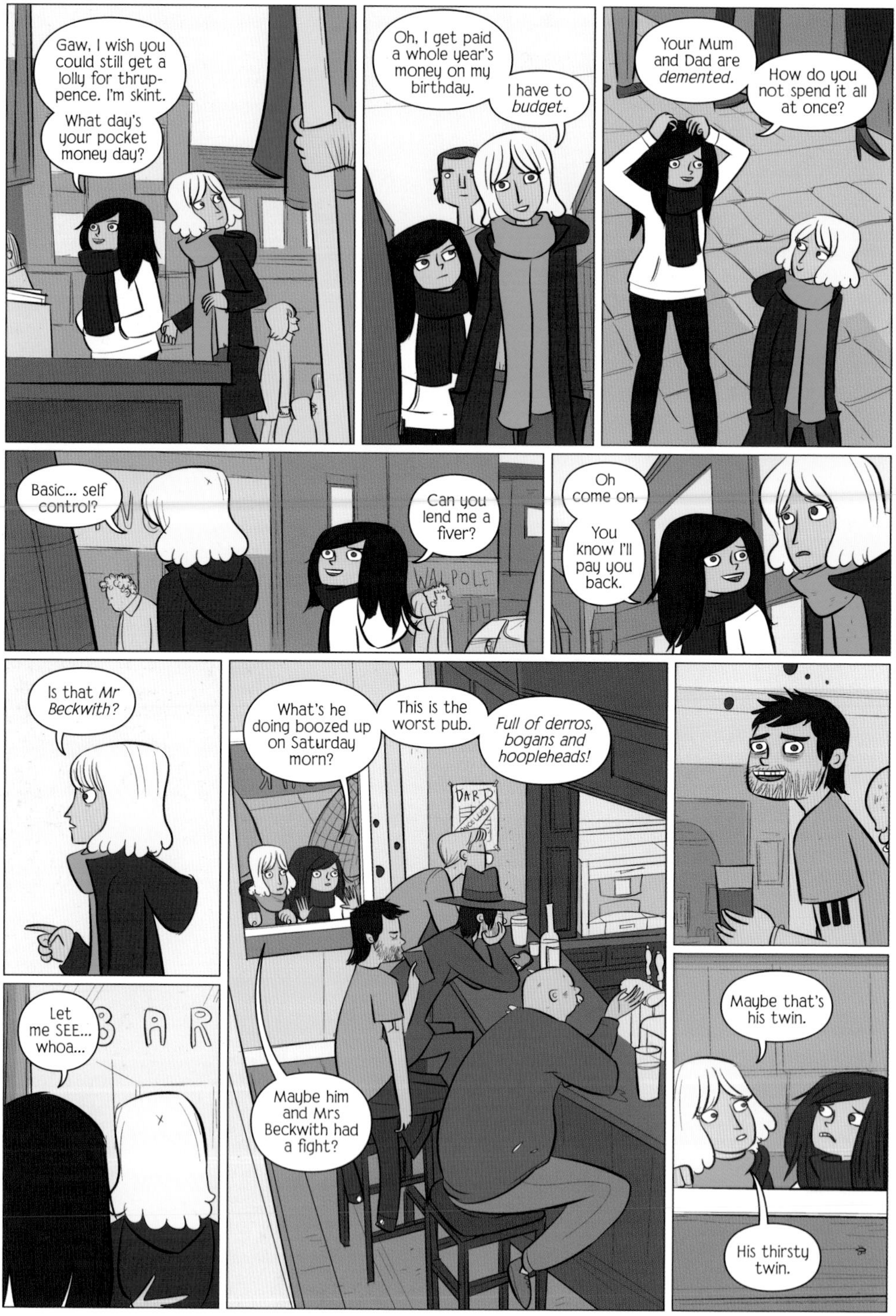
Gaw, I wish you could still get a lolly for thrup-pence. I'm skint.
What day's your pocket money day?
Oh, I get paid a whole year's money on my birthday.
I have to *budget*.
Your Mum and Dad are *demented*.
How do you not spend it all at once?
Basic... self control?
Can you lend me a fiver?
WALPOLE
Oh come on.
You know I'll pay you back.
Is that *Mr Beckwith?*
Let me SEE... whoa...
BAR
What's he doing boozed up on Saturday morn?
This is the worst pub.
Full of derros, bogans and hoopleheads!
DARTS
Maybe him and Mrs Beckwith had a fight?
Maybe that's his twin.
His thirsty twin.

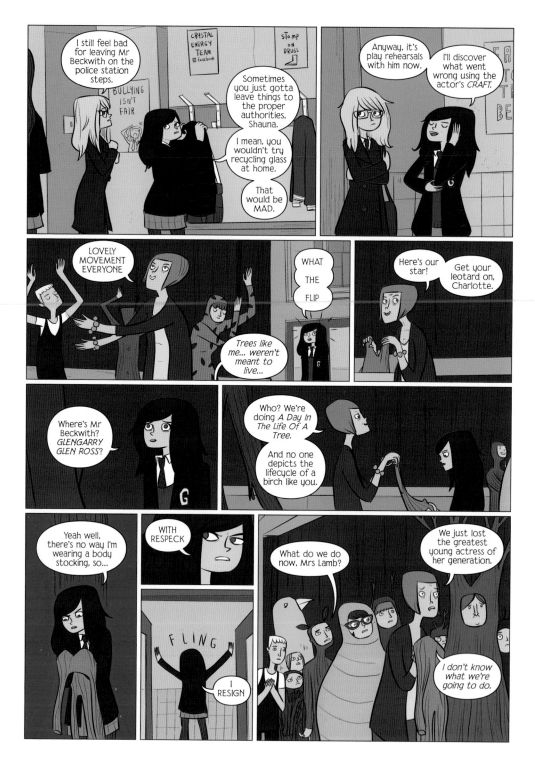

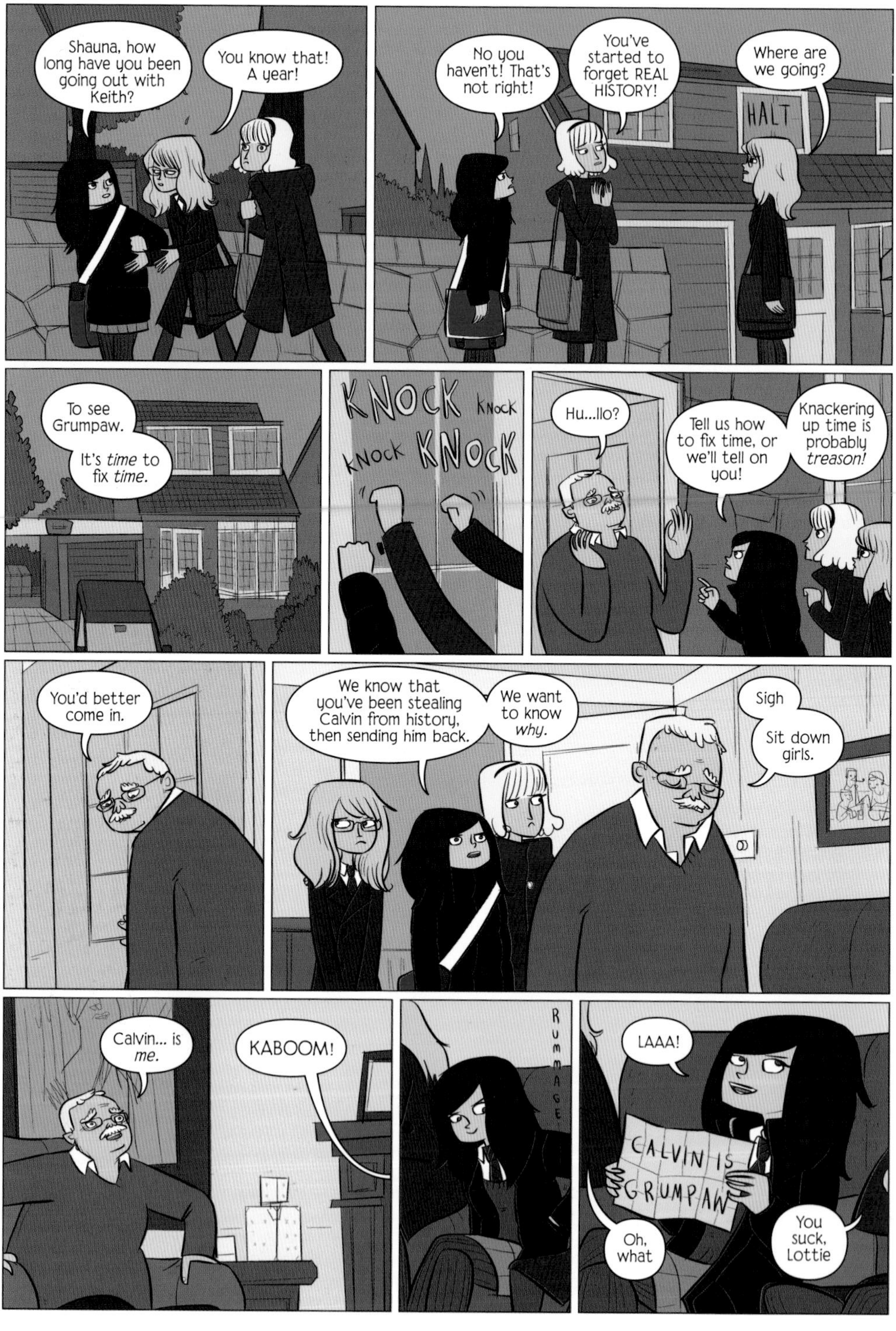
Shauna, how long have you been going out with Keith?
You know that! A year!
No you haven't! That's not right!
You've started to forget REAL HISTORY!
Where are we going?
HALT
To see Grumpaw.
It's *time* to fix *time*.
KNOCK KNOCK KNOCK KNOCK
Hu...llo?
Tell us how to fix time, or we'll tell on you!
Knackering up time is probably *treason!*
You'd better come in.
We know that you've been stealing Calvin from history, then sending him back.
We want to know *why*.
Sigh
Sit down girls.
Calvin... is *me*.
KABOOM!
RUMMAGE
LAAA!
CALVIN IS GRUMPAW
Oh, what
You suck, Lottie

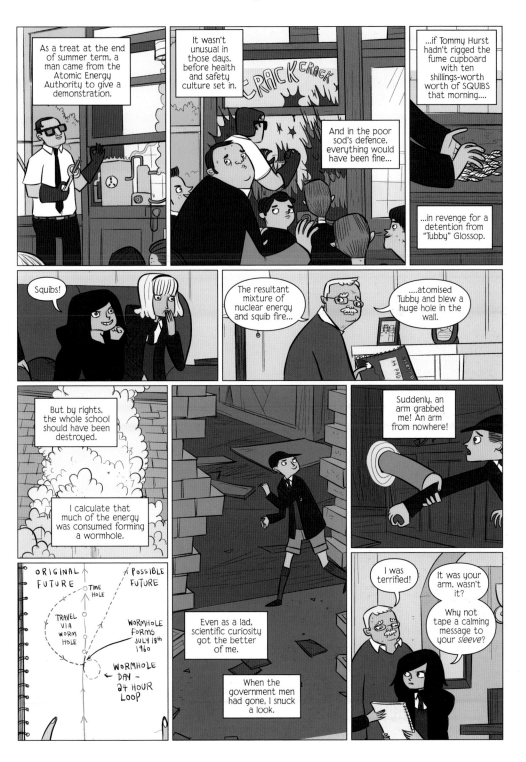

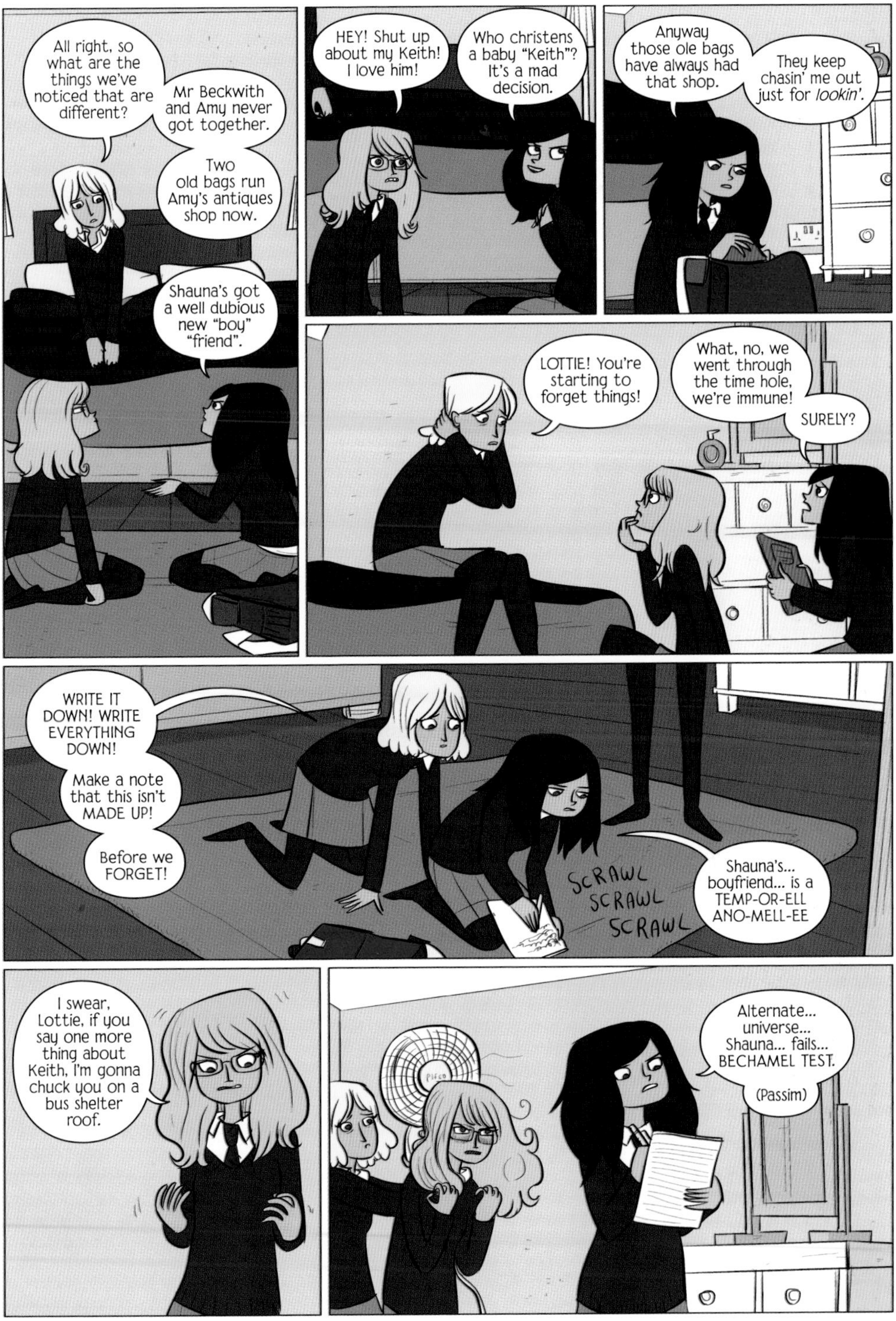
All right, so what are the things we've noticed that are different?
Mr Beckwith and Amy never got together.
Two old bags run Amy's antiques shop now.
Shauna's got a well dubious new "boy" "friend".
HEY! Shut up about my Keith! I love him!
Who christens a baby "Keith"? It's a mad decision.
Anyway those ole bags have always had that shop.
They keep chasin' me out just for *lookin'*.
LOTTIE! You're starting to forget things!
What, no, we went through the time hole, we're immune!
SURELY?
WRITE IT DOWN! WRITE EVERYTHING DOWN!
Make a note that this isn't MADE UP!
Before we FORGET!
SCRAWL SCRAWL SCRAWL
Shauna's... boyfriend... is a TEMP-OR-ELL ANO-MELL-EE
I swear, Lottie, if you say one more thing about Keith, I'm gonna chuck you on a bus shelter roof.
Alternate... universe... Shauna... fails... BECHAMEL TEST.
(Passim)

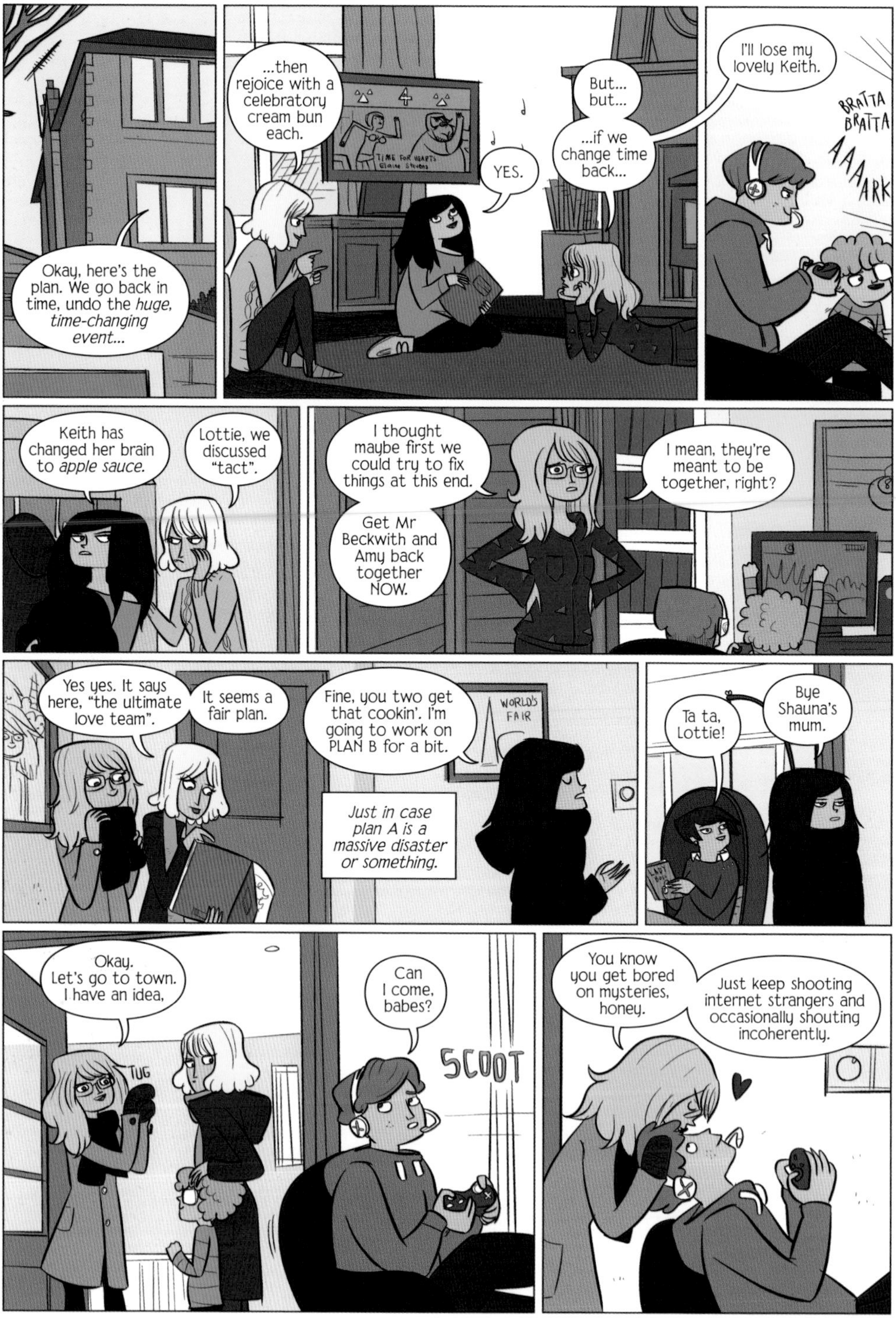
Okay, here's the plan. We go back in time, undo the *huge, time-changing event...*
...then rejoice with a celebratory cream bun each.
TIME FOR HEARTS
YES.
But... but...
...if we change time back...
I'll lose my lovely Keith.
BRATTA BRATTA
AAAARK
Keith has changed her brain to *apple sauce.*
Lottie, we discussed "tact".
I thought maybe first we could try to fix things at this end.
Get Mr Beckwith and Amy back together NOW.
I mean, they're meant to be together, right?
Yes yes. It says here, "the ultimate love team".
It seems a fair plan.
Fine, you two get that cookin'. I'm going to work on PLAN B for a bit.
WORLD'S FAIR
Just in case plan A is a massive disaster or something.
Ta ta, Lottie!
Bye Shauna's mum.
Okay. Let's go to town. I have an idea.
TUG
Can I come, babes?
SCOOT
You know you get bored on mysteries, honey.
Just keep shooting internet strangers and occasionally shouting incoherently.

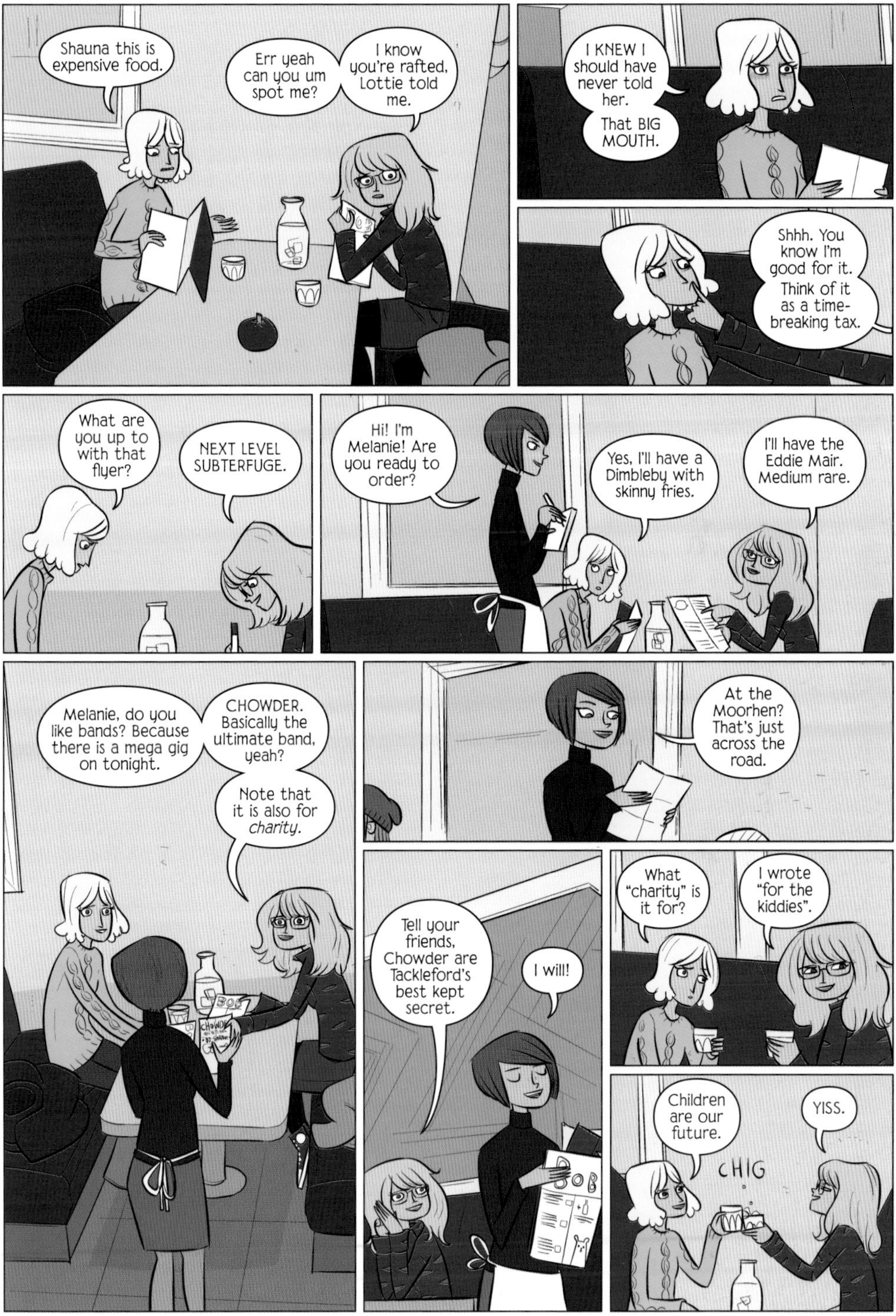
Shauna this is expensive food.
Err yeah can you um spot me?
I know you're rafted, Lottie told me.
I KNEW I should have never told her.
That BIG MOUTH.
Shhh. You know I'm good for it.
Think of it as a time-breaking tax.
What are you up to with that flyer?
NEXT LEVEL SUBTERFUGE.
Hi! I'm Melanie! Are you ready to order?
Yes, I'll have a Dimbleby with skinny fries.
I'll have the Eddie Mair. Medium rare.
Melanie, do you like bands? Because there is a mega gig on tonight.
CHOWDER. Basically the ultimate band, yeah?
Note that it is also for *charity*.
At the Moorhen? That's just across the road.
Tell your friends, Chowder are Tackleford's best kept secret.
I will!
What "charity" is it for?
I wrote "for the kiddies".
Children are our future.
YISS.
CHIG

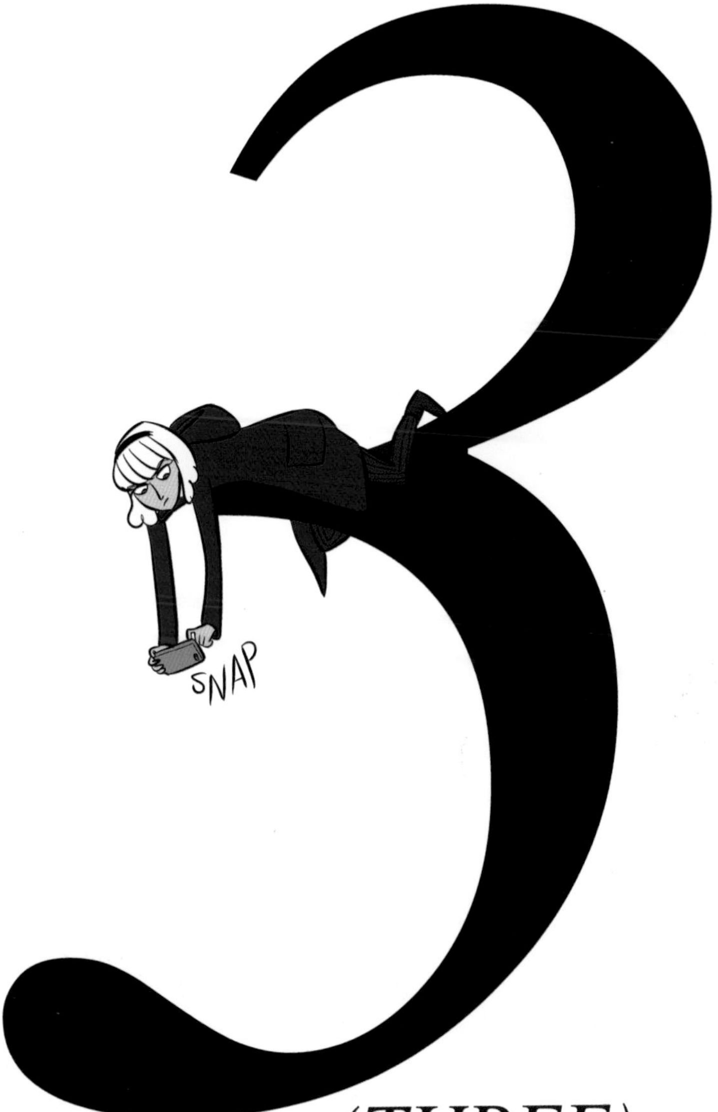
SNAP

3 (THREE)

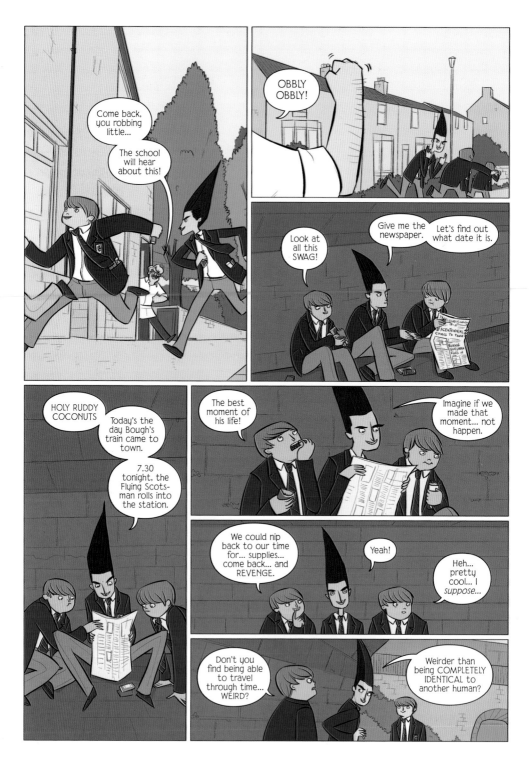

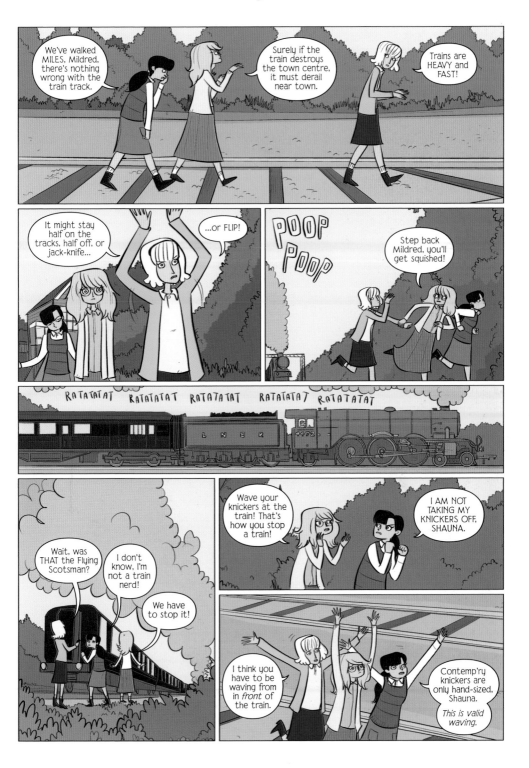

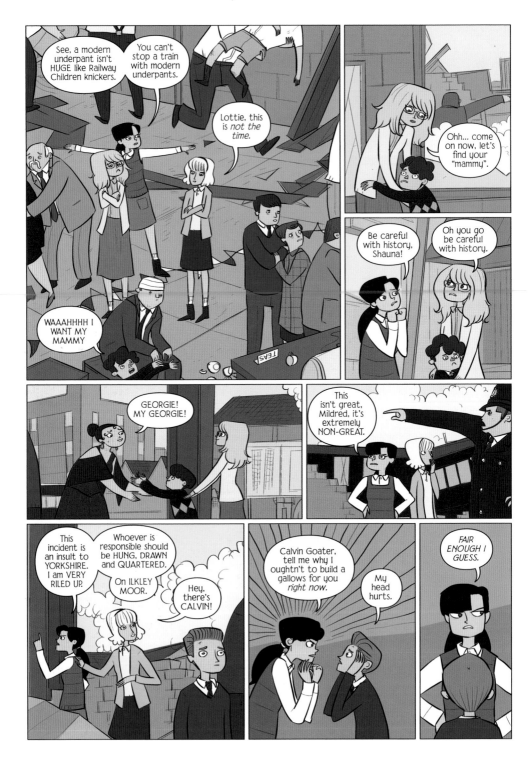

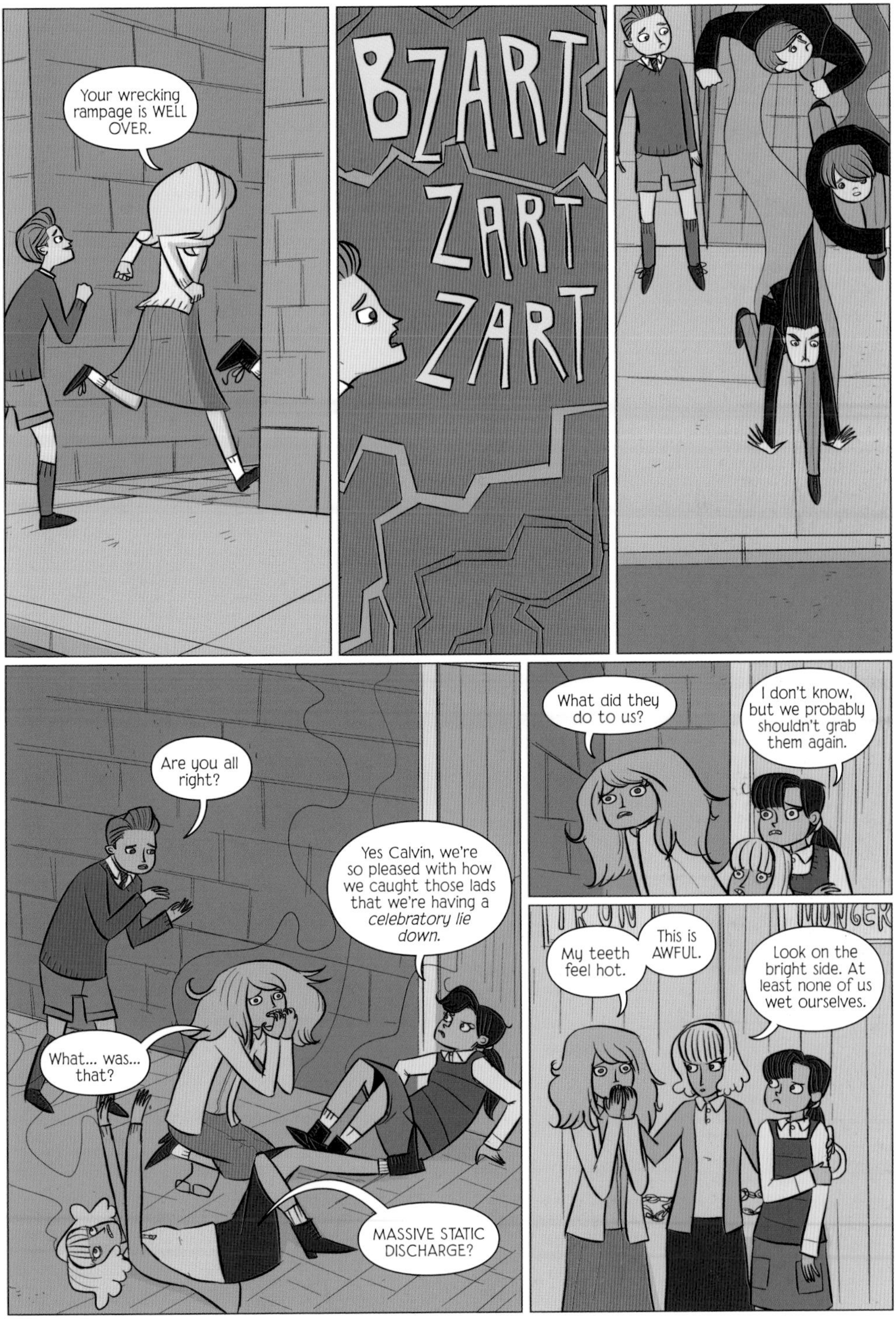
Your wrecking rampage is WELL OVER.
BZART
ZART
ZART
Are you all right?
Yes Calvin, we're so pleased with how we caught those lads that we're having a *celebratory lie down.*
What... was... that?
MASSIVE STATIC DISCHARGE?
What did they do to us?
I don't know, but we probably shouldn't grab them again.
My teeth feel hot.
This is AWFUL.
Look on the bright side. At least none of us wet ourselves.

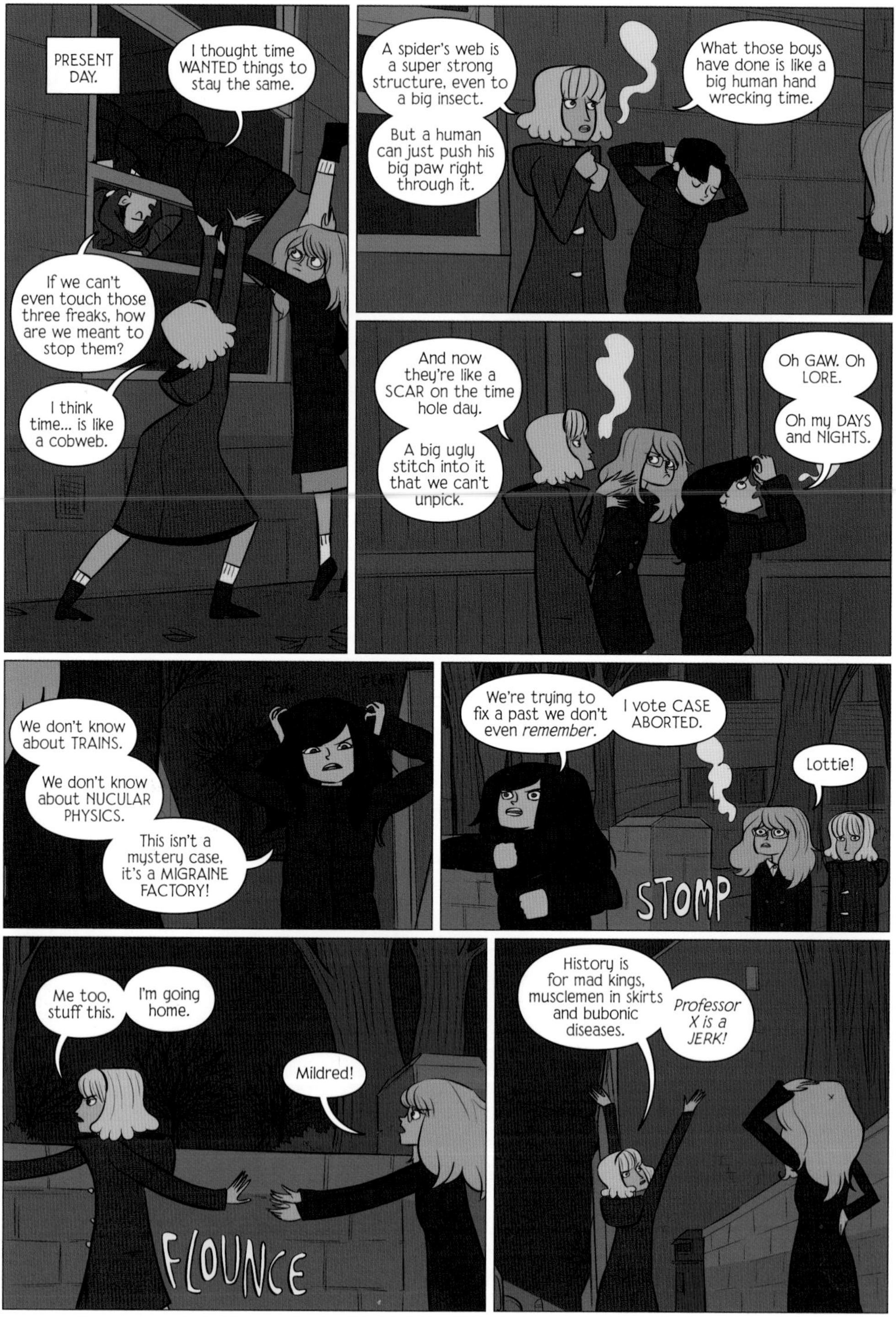
PRESENT DAY.
I thought time WANTED things to stay the same.
If we can't even touch those three freaks, how are we meant to stop them?
I think time... is like a cobweb.
A spider's web is a super strong structure, even to a big insect.
But a human can just push his big paw right through it.
What those boys have done is like a big human hand wrecking time.
And now they're like a SCAR on the time hole day.
A big ugly stitch into it that we can't unpick.
Oh GAW. Oh LORE.
Oh my DAYS and NIGHTS.
We don't know about TRAINS.
We don't know about NUCULAR PHYSICS.
This isn't a mystery case, it's a MIGRAINE FACTORY!
We're trying to fix a past we don't even *remember*.
I vote CASE ABORTED.
Lottie!
STOMP
Me too, stuff this.
I'm going home.
Mildred!
FLOUNCE
History is for mad kings, musclemen in skirts and bubonic diseases.
Professor X is a JERK!

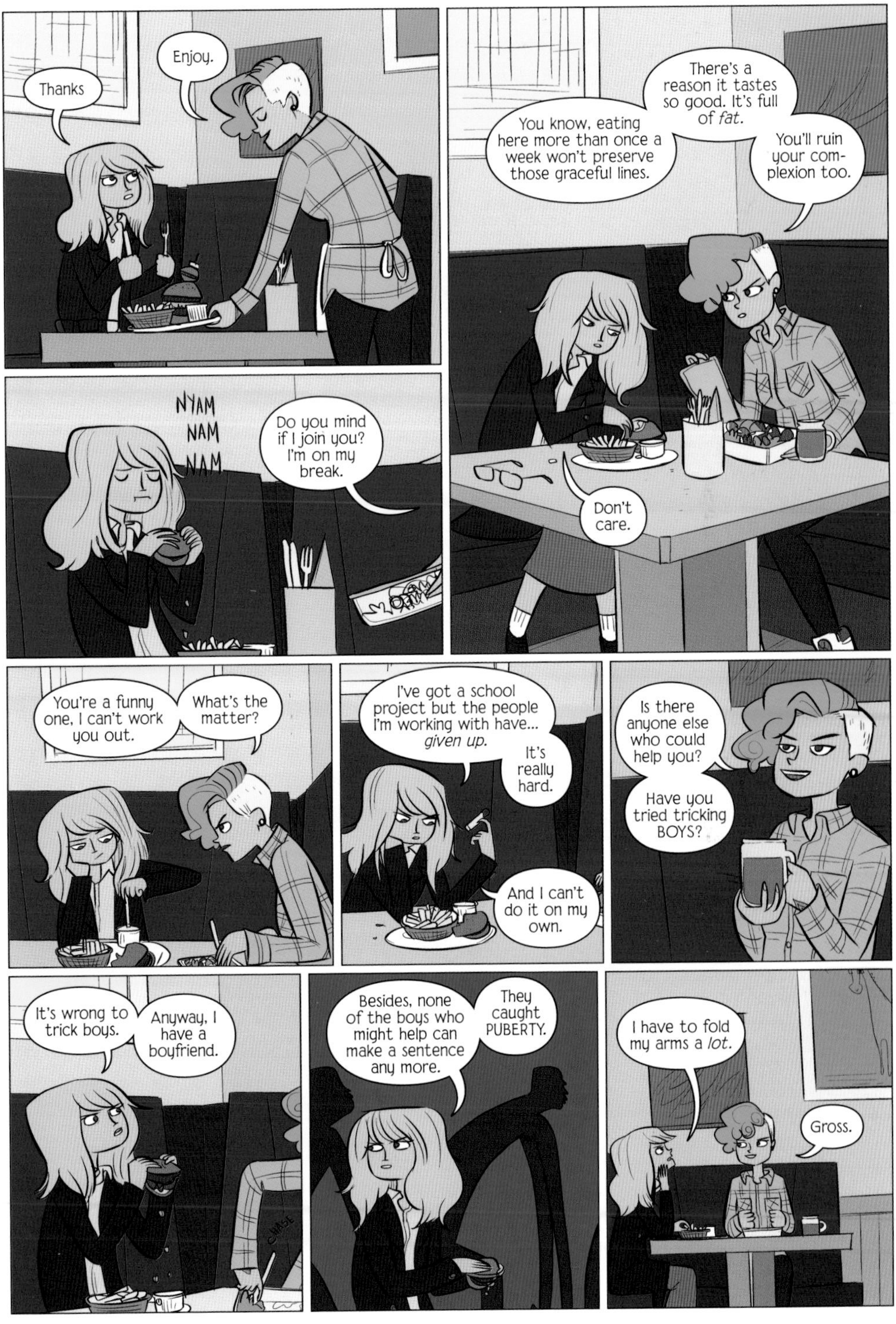
Thanks
Enjoy.
You know, eating here more than once a week won't preserve those graceful lines.
There's a reason it tastes so good. It's full of *fat.*
You'll ruin your complexion too.
NYAM NAM NAM
Do you mind if I join you? I'm on my break.
Don't care.
You're a funny one, I can't work you out.
What's the matter?
I've got a school project but the people I'm working with have... *given up.*
It's really hard.
And I can't do it on my own.
Is there anyone else who could help you?
Have you tried tricking BOYS?
It's wrong to trick boys.
Anyway, I have a boyfriend.
Besides, none of the boys who might help can make a sentence any more.
They caught PUBERTY.
I have to fold my arms a *lot.*
Gross.

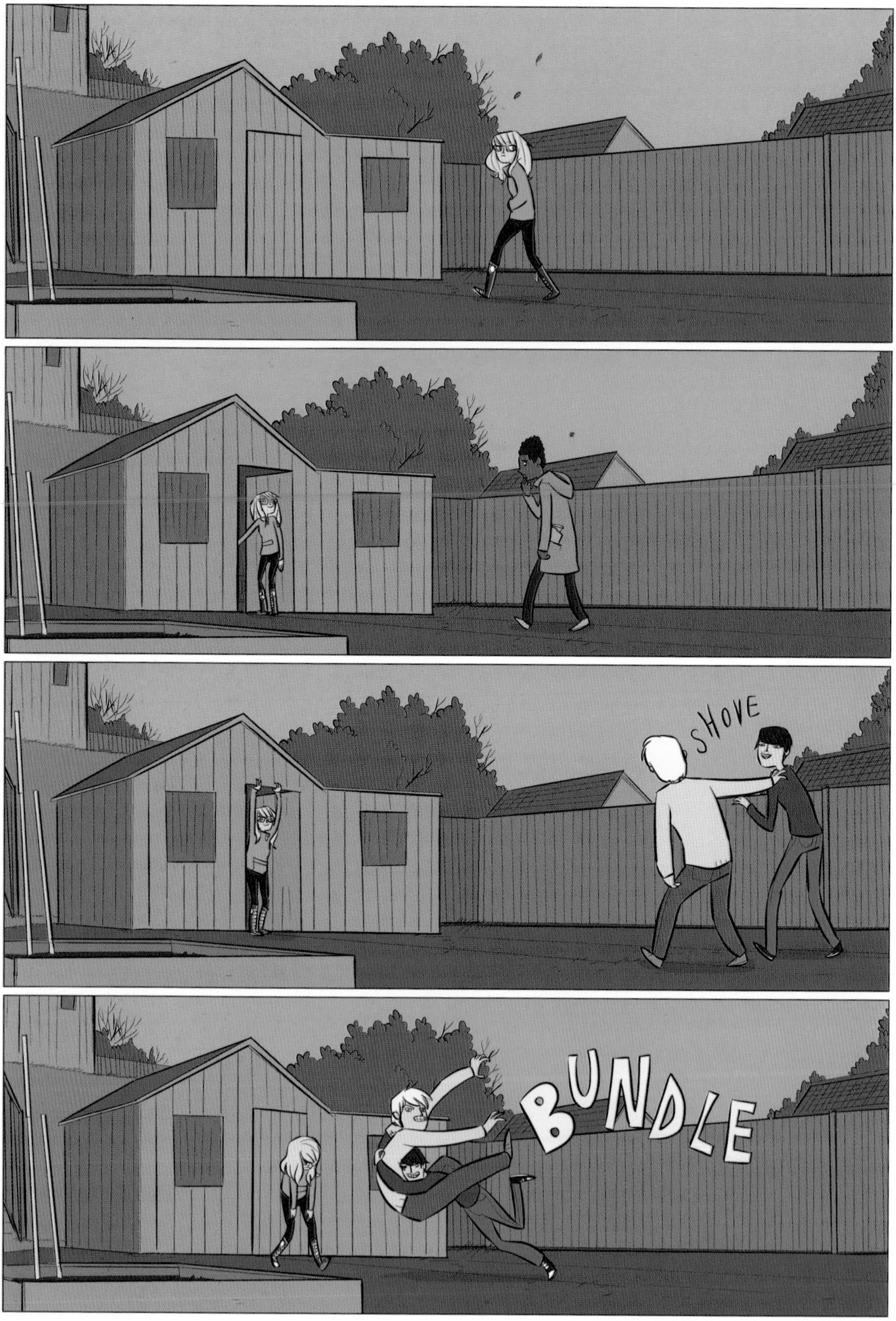
SHOVE
BUNDLE

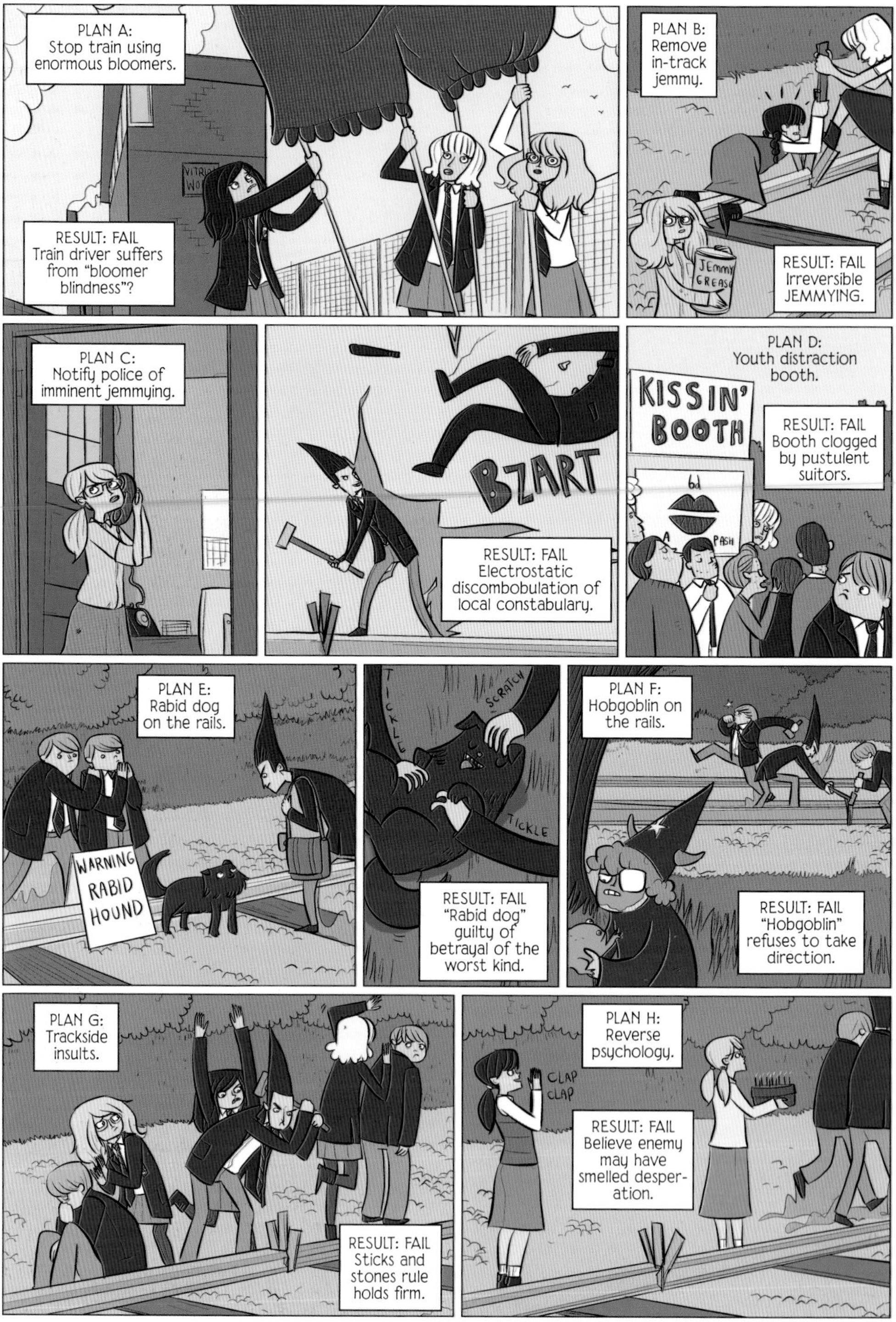
PLAN A: Stop train using enormous bloomers.
VITRIO WO
RESULT: FAIL Train driver suffers from "bloomer blindness"?
PLAN B: Remove in-track jemmy.
JEMMY GREASE
RESULT: FAIL Irreversible JEMMYING.
PLAN C: Notify police of imminent jemmying.
BZART
RESULT: FAIL Electrostatic discombobulation of local constabulary.
PLAN D: Youth distraction booth.
KISSIN' BOOTH
RESULT: FAIL Booth clogged by pustulent suitors.
6d
A
PASH
PLAN E: Rabid dog on the rails.
WARNING RABID HOUND
TICKLE
SCRATCH
TICKLE
RESULT: FAIL "Rabid dog" guilty of betrayal of the worst kind.
PLAN F: Hobgoblin on the rails.
RESULT: FAIL "Hobgoblin" refuses to take direction.
PLAN G: Trackside insults.
RESULT: FAIL Sticks and stones rule holds firm.
PLAN H: Reverse psychology.
CLAP CLAP
RESULT: FAIL Believe enemy may have smelled desper-ation.

98

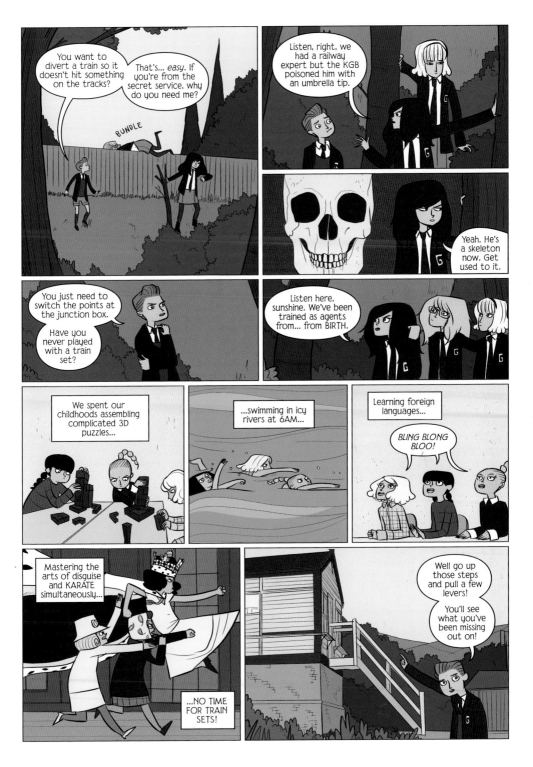

We could tell the rail men about aromatherapy.

That's gotta rock a few worlds in these primitive times.

"Smell and be well!"

NO.

I've got an idea. Those men probably fought in the war!

Go on Calvin.

If you tell them that the town is in danger...

...that a symbol of Great Britain is about to be destroyed....

Yes yes, keep going, this is good...

WEFFUS-N   Q19
LIGHT   STOPWATCH
Hi Ω   COUNTDOWN
00:10:13
MODE   50 METRE

...by agents of the USSR acting on behalf of Stalin's ghost...

...they'll help!

Let me go up and tell them.

Wait Calvin! I'll do it.

But I want to see the *levers*.

I'll ask them if you can have a look.

What do you think she's actually going to say to them?

Hopefully nothing about STALIN's GHOST hem hem.

She might just be going to cadge a cup of tea.

Wickle's a right old tea bag.

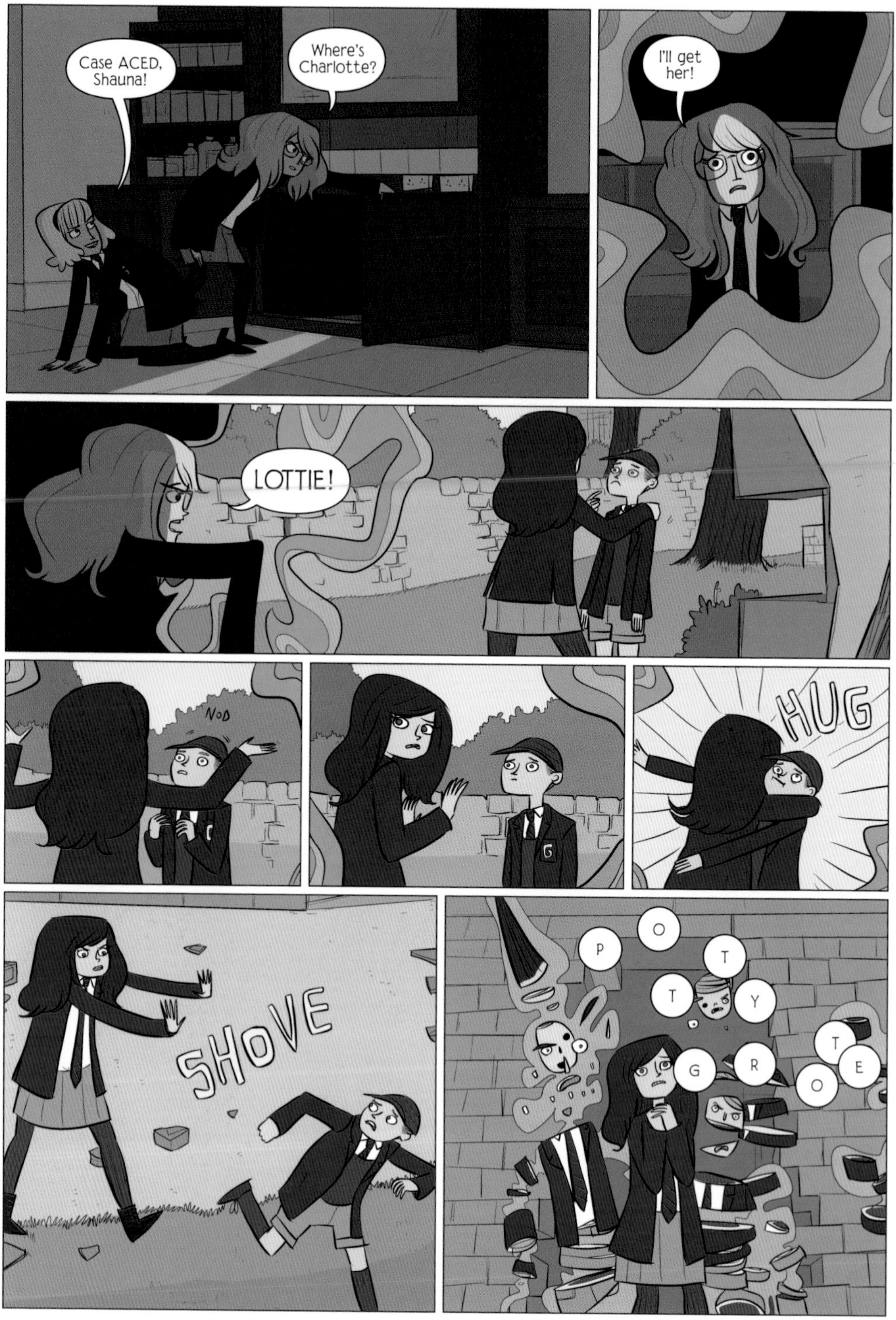
Case ACED, Shauna!
Where's Charlotte?
I'll get her!
LOTTIE!
NOD
HUG
SHOVE
P
O
T
T
Y
G
R
O
T
E

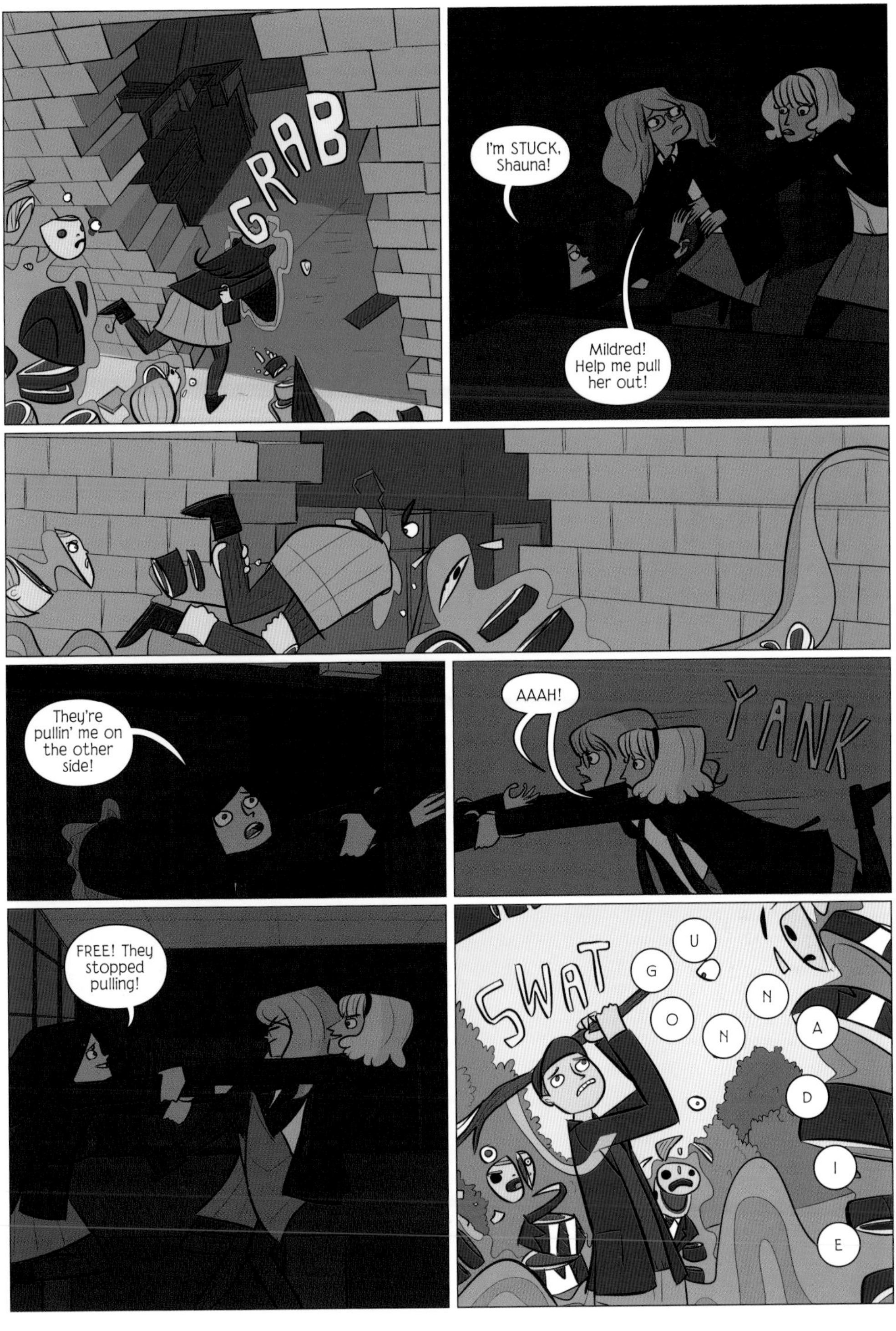
GRAB
I'm STUCK, Shauna!
Mildred! Help me pull her out!
They're pullin' me on the other side!
AAAH!
YANK
FREE! They stopped pulling!
SWAT
G
U
O
N
N
A
D
I
E

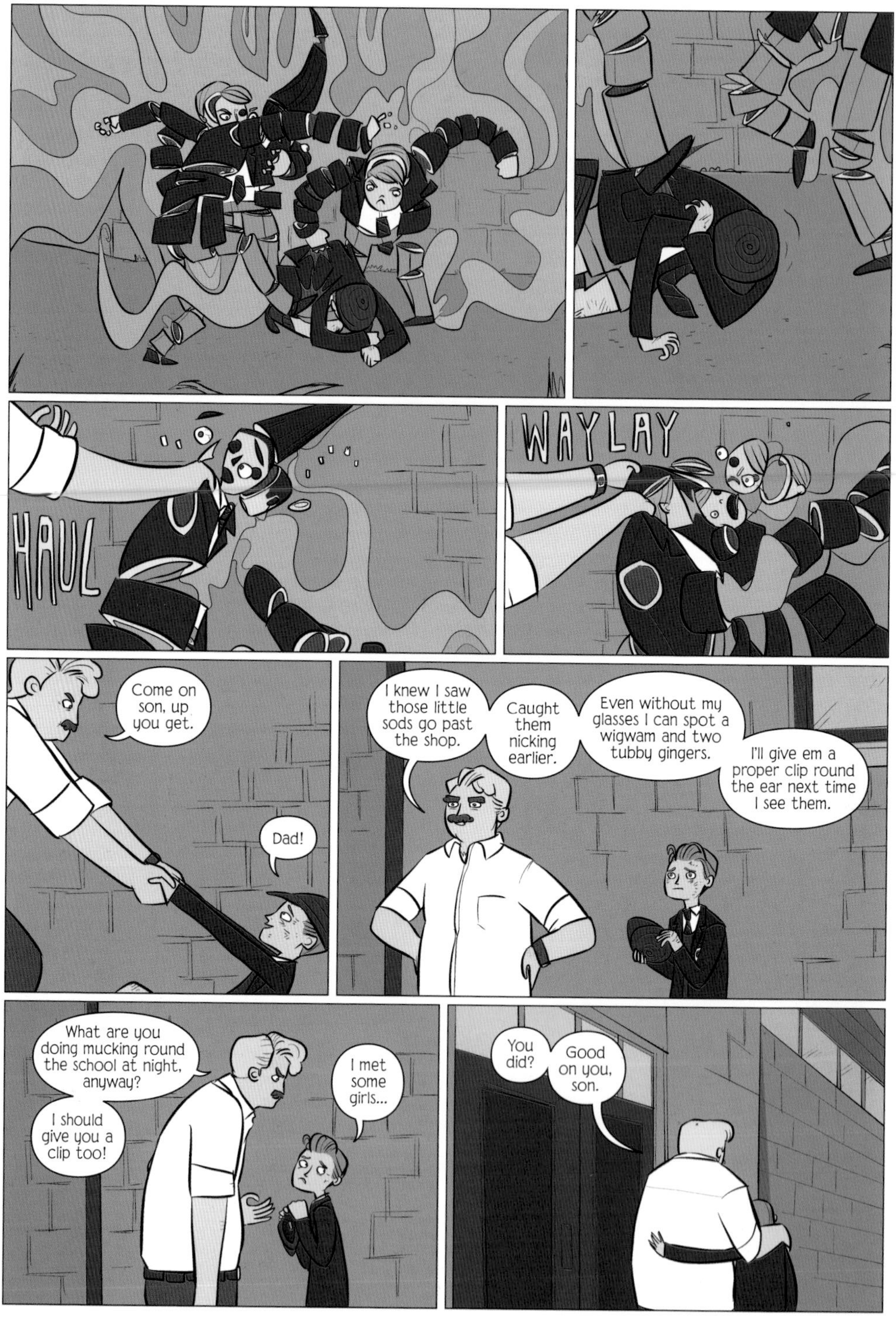
HAUL
WAYLAY
Come on son, up you get.
Dad!
I knew I saw those little sods go past the shop.
Caught them nicking earlier.
Even without my glasses I can spot a wigwam and two tubby gingers.
I'll give em a proper clip round the ear next time I see them.
What are you doing mucking round the school at night, anyway?
I should give you a clip too!
I met some girls...
You did?
Good on you, son.

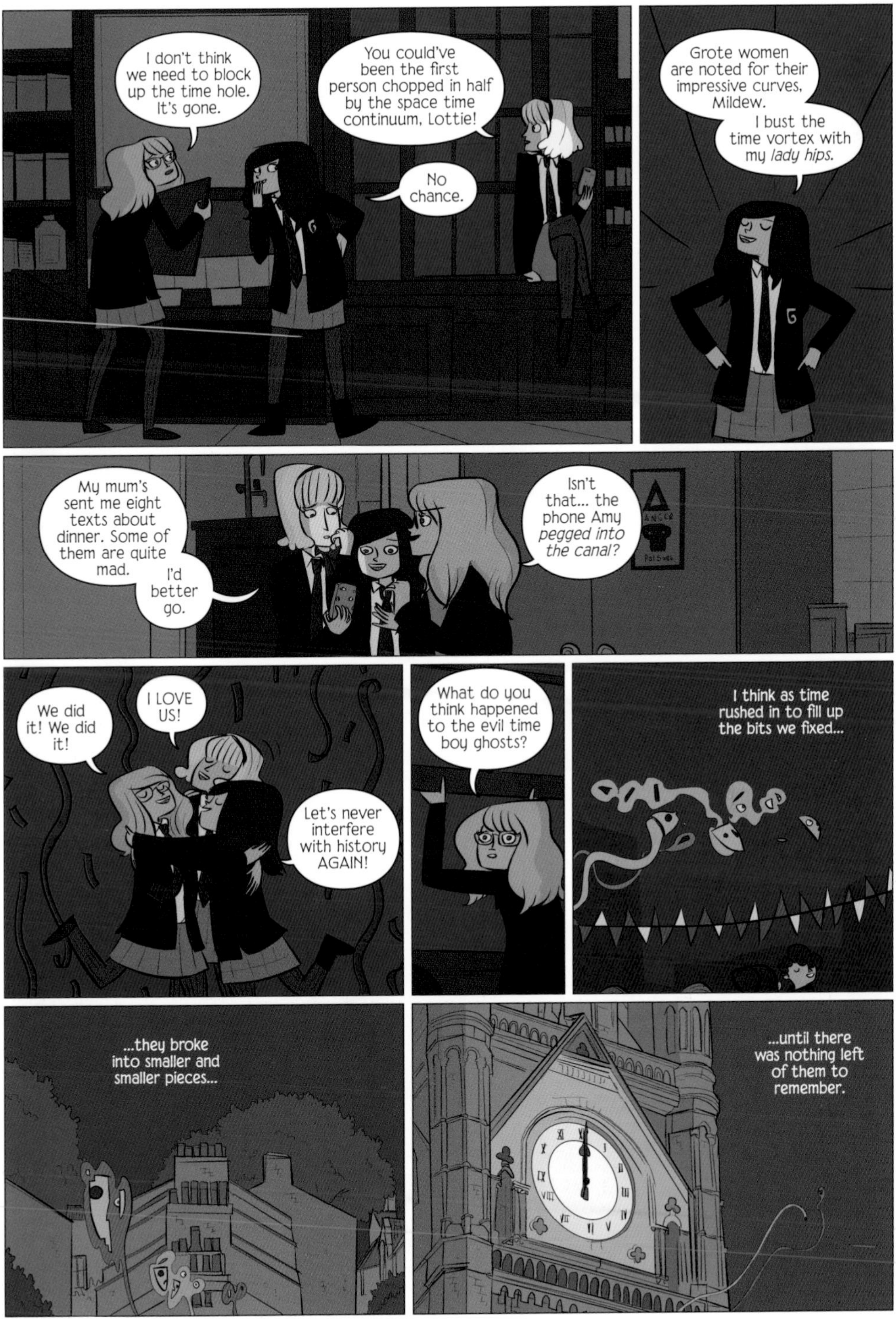
I don't think we need to block up the time hole. It's gone.
You could've been the first person chopped in half by the space time continuum, Lottie!
No chance.
Grote women are noted for their impressive curves, Mildew.
I bust the time vortex with my *lady hips*.
My mum's sent me eight texts about dinner. Some of them are quite mad.
I'd better go.
Isn't that... the phone Amy *pegged into the canal?*
We did it! We did it!
I LOVE US!
Let's never interfere with history AGAIN!
What do you think happened to the evil time boy ghosts?
I think as time rushed in to fill up the bits we fixed...
...they broke into smaller and smaller pieces...
...until there was nothing left of them to remember.

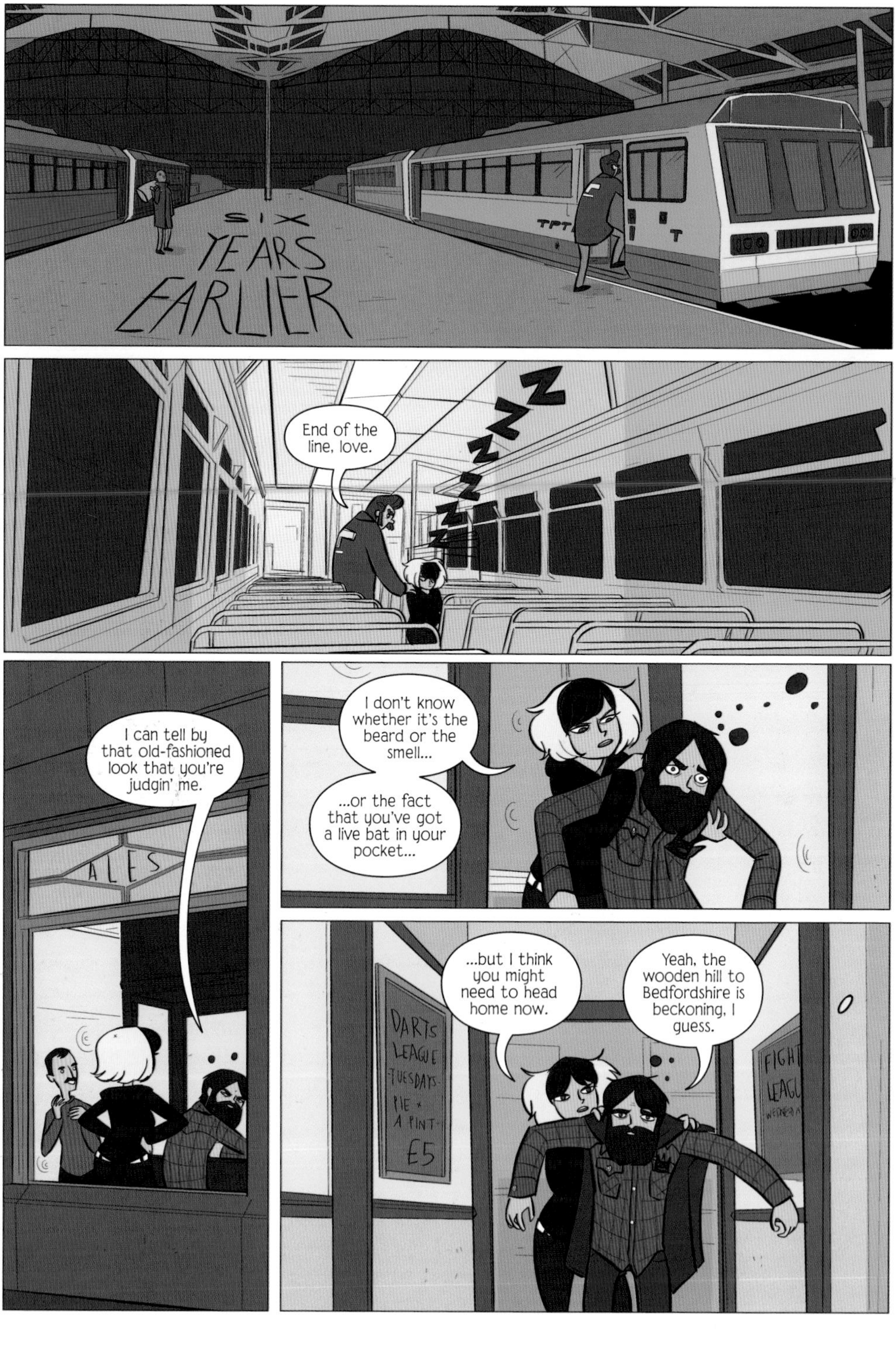
SIX YEARS EARLIER
TPT
End of the line, love.
ZZZZZZZ
I can tell by that old-fashioned look that you're judgin' me.
ALES
I don't know whether it's the beard or the smell...
...or the fact that you've got a live bat in your pocket...
...but I think you might need to head home now.
Yeah, the wooden hill to Bedfordshire is beckoning, I guess.
DARTS LEAGUE TUESDAYS PIE + A PINT £5
FIGHT LEAGU

(FIN)

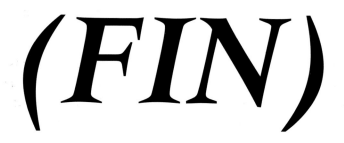

BACK IN TINE*: THE HISTORY OF THE FORKED ROAD

You know, like the prongs on a fork, look it up in a dictionary

Thank you for buying and reading *The Case Of The Forked Road*. I know what you are thinking. You are thinking, "I would have paid twice as much for this book" (if you bought it) or "I should buy the librarian a cream cake" if you got it from a library or "why are all the shop staff looking at me funny" if you have read the whole thing in your local book shop. It is that good.

But *Bad Machinery* number seven is not just a fun and scientifically confused journey into great acting, romance confusion, deodorant and "the timestream". It is also a tale that touches some important moments in Tackleford's past, namely the love and friendship of Mr and Mrs Ryan & Amy Beckwith-Chilton. Before they were A) a teacher with a suspicious love of elbow patches and B) a queenly antiques woman, they were just confused humans barely capable of tying their own shoelaces, or so I hear.

They had a lot of adventures, together and apart, before they decided to kiss each other's faces over and over again and do a marriage. And the critical events of this case revisit some important points that were first shown to the public in the historical and unimportant comic strip "Scary Go Round".

So over the next few pages, please enjoy a selection of the magic moments that follow Amy's fateful finding of the bearded Beckwith. It's the moment that turned them from two people who never knew where their next clean pair of socks were coming from, into the kind of upstanding humans who a bank manager would lend the money to buy a house with.

I have added some notes with my own thoughts under these comics, just a few basic opinions. Only v. mildly controversial.

NOW READ ON!

Charlotte Grote
Tackleford, UK.

THE BAT IS EATING ACORNS

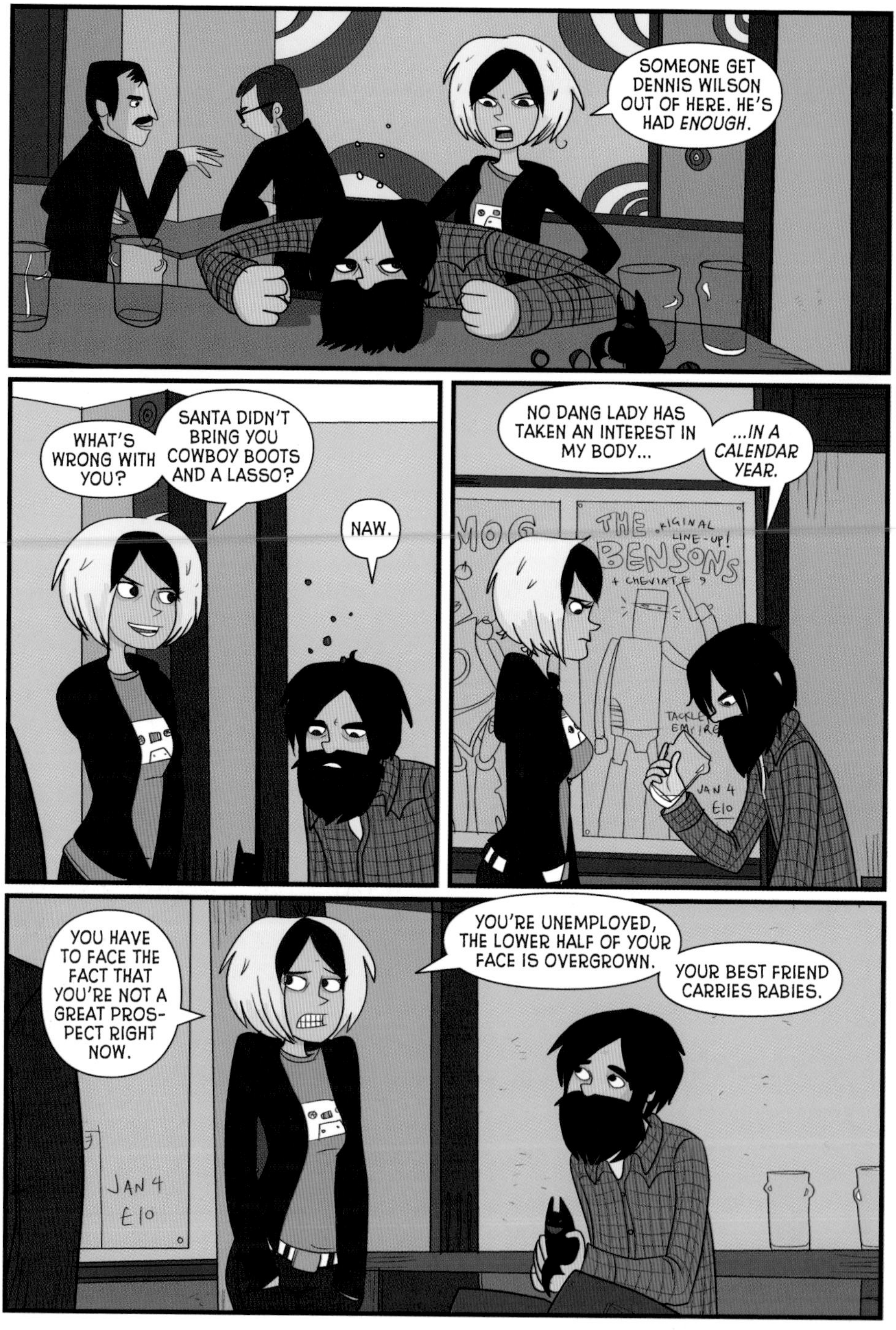

SOMEONE GET DENNIS WILSON OUT OF HERE. HE'S HAD *ENOUGH*.
WHAT'S WRONG WITH YOU?
SANTA DIDN'T BRING YOU COWBOY BOOTS AND A LASSO?
NAW.
NO DANG LADY HAS TAKEN AN INTEREST IN MY BODY...
...IN A CALENDAR YEAR.
THE BENSONS
ORIGINAL LINE-UP!
+ CHEVIATE
JAN 4
£10
YOU HAVE TO FACE THE FACT THAT YOU'RE NOT A GREAT PROSPECT RIGHT NOW.
YOU'RE UNEMPLOYED, THE LOWER HALF OF YOUR FACE IS OVERGROWN.
YOUR BEST FRIEND CARRIES RABIES.
JAN 4
£10

Dennis Wilson was the drummer in the Beach Boys. He pretty much invented the idea of being cool and having a beard. You will note that Ryan has a pet bat. This is totally against the law. That was the kind of man he was. A rebel. Or an idiot. But the bat seems to like it so I guess he knew what he was doing. Maybe they just "found each other".

A LOAD OF EXCESS

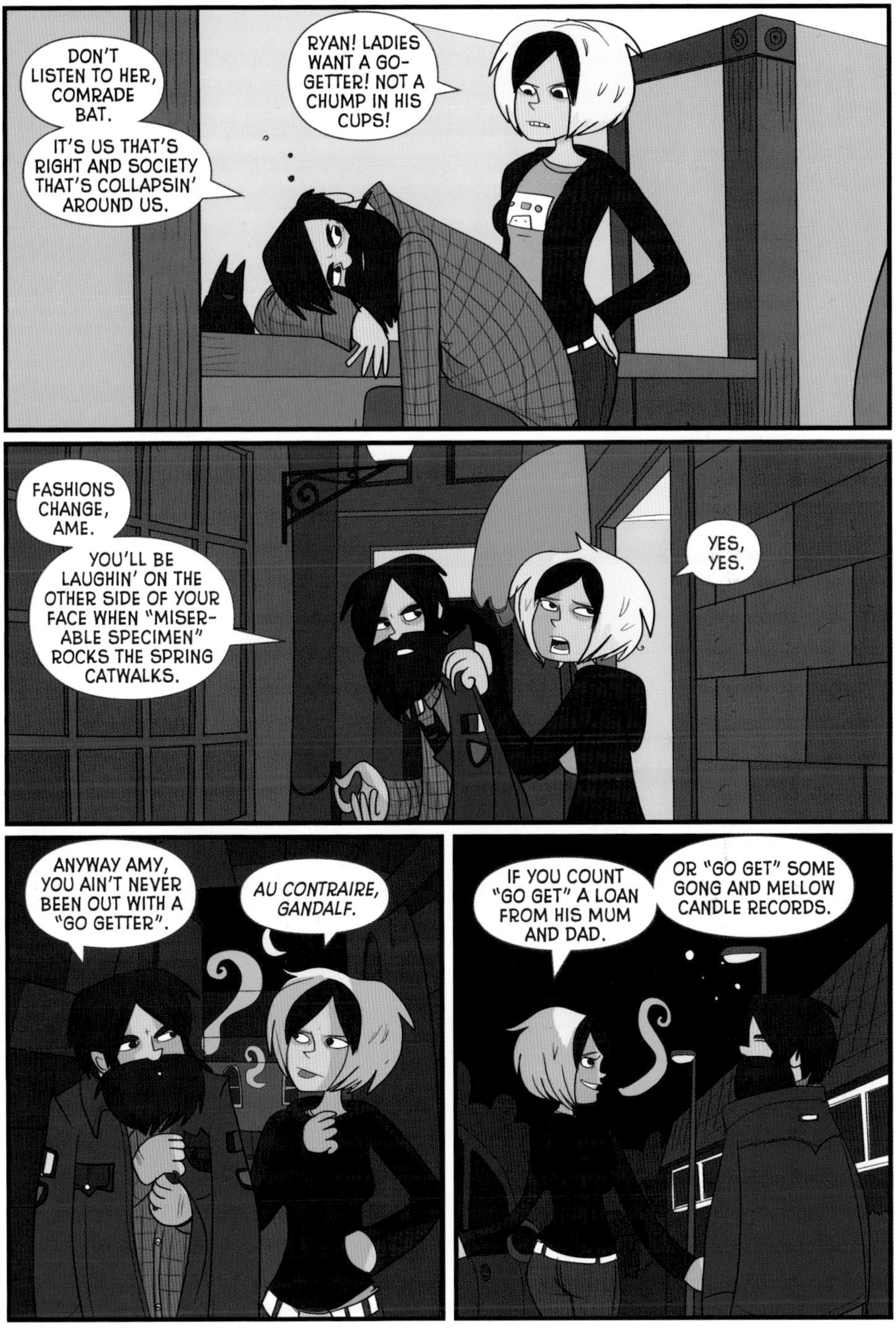

DON'T LISTEN TO HER, COMRADE BAT.
IT'S US THAT'S RIGHT AND SOCIETY THAT'S COLLAPSIN' AROUND US.
RYAN! LADIES WANT A GO-GETTER! NOT A CHUMP IN HIS CUPS!
FASHIONS CHANGE, AME.
YOU'LL BE LAUGHIN' ON THE OTHER SIDE OF YOUR FACE WHEN "MISER-ABLE SPECIMEN" ROCKS THE SPRING CATWALKS.
YES, YES.
ANYWAY AMY, YOU AIN'T NEVER BEEN OUT WITH A "GO GETTER".
AU CONTRAIRE, GANDALF.
IF YOU COUNT "GO GET" A LOAN FROM HIS MUM AND DAD.
OR "GO GET" SOME GONG AND MELLOW CANDLE RECORDS.

This comic was written before everybody got a beard. You can't laugh at people with beards now. If Amy was a single lady on the go in any major metropolis, she'd be noting down the beards in her beard book for future reference. It's what a dame does these days. There are so many kinds. There's greasy, disgusting, barely presentable, over-fancy, and bearable. Beards are a full time job.

THE ROAD TO SUCCESS

This comic makes reference to my mentor and guide Shelley Winters, who was not around at this point, being on a global trip (I reckon, anyway). She is well a jet setter, and my idol. Weirdly she has never appeared in a mystery case, but her younger sister, Erin Winters, is in loads of them. Shelley is gentle and kind, unlike her sister, who (as you may recall), spends her days mis-spelling my name for fun. She's an awful person.

CLASSIC CRONES

The awful old bags in this strip show up when Shauna goes to Amy's shop after time gets changed and things go wrong. They're a right pair. Around this time they burned Amy's shop down, which I suppose made a change from selling jigsaw puzzles with missing bits and hideous porcelain clowns. They have not been seen around town for years, but sometimes you can smell them... on the breeze.

MELANIE SOAP

An important figure in this story is Miss Melanie (who appears in the very first mystery case, but then seems to vanish). Melanie was totally sweet on Ryan back in the day, she thought he hung the moon in the sky. As you can see, her Pop is a magistrate and a dangerous loon obsessed with pirates etc, so Ryan probably felt it was safer to seek love with Amy. I cannot argue with this decision. She's a total peach! But I hope Miss Melanie has found a special someone, somewhere. She's a peach too.

JOHN ALLISON

Born in a hidden village deep within the British Alps, John Allison came into this world a respectable baby with style and taste. Having been exposed to American comics at an early age, he spent decades honing his keen mind and his massive body in order to burn out this colonial cultural infection.

One of the longest continuously publishing independent web-based cartoonists, John has plied his trade since the late nineties moving from *Bobbins* to *Scary Go Round* to *Bad Machinery,* developing the deeply weird world of Tackleford long after many of his fellow artists were ground into dust and bones by Time Itself.

He has only once shed a single tear, but you only meet Sergio Aragonés for the first time once.

John resides in Letchworth Garden City, England, and is known to his fellow villagers only as He Who Has Conquered.

—Contributed by Richard Stevens III

"THE TREASURE OF BRITANNIA"

ALSO FROM JOHN ALLISON & ONI PRESS

BAD MACHINERY, VOLUME 1:
THE CASE OF THE TEAM SPIRIT
ISBN 978-1-62010-387-6
Pocket Edition In Stores Now!

BAD MACHINERY, VOLUME 2:
THE CASE OF THE GOOD BOY
ISBN 978-1-62010-421-7
Pocket Edition In Stores Now!

BAD MACHINERY, VOLUME 3:
THE CASE OF THE SIMPLE SOUL
ISBN 978-1-62010-443-9
Pocket Edition In Stores Now!

BAD MACHINERY, VOLUME 4:
THE CASE OF THE LONELY ONE
ISBN 978-1-62010-457-6
Pocket Edition In Stores Now!

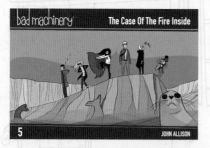

BAD MACHINERY, VOLUME 5:
THE CASE OF THE FIRE INSIDE
ISBN 978-1-62010-504-7
Pocket Edition In Stores Now!

BAD MACHINERY, VOLUME 6:
THE CASE OF THE UNWELCOME VISITOR
ISBN 978-1-62010-543-6
Pocket Edition In Stores Now!

bad machinery
THE CASE OF THE MODERN MEN

Coming Summer 2019!